MUMMIES, DINOSAURS, MOON ROCKS

HOW WE KNOW HOW OLD THINGS ARE

by James Jespersen and Jane Fitz-Randolph

Illustrated by Bruce Hiscock and with photographs

ATHENEUM BOOKS FOR YOUNG READERS

FOR
DONALD EUGENE MYLANDER
AND
KENNETH JOE BRUCHEZ

Atheneum Books for Young Readers
An imprint of Simon & Schuster Children's Publishing Division
1230 Avenue of the Americas
New York, New York 10020

Designed by Anne Scatto/PIXEL PRESS
The text of this book is set in Goudy Old Style.
The illustrations are rendered in pen & ink.
Printed in the United States.

10 9 8 7 6 5 4 3 2 1

Library of Congress Cataloging-in-Publication Data
Jespersen, James.
Mummies, dinosaurs, moon rocks : how we know how old things are / by James Jespersen and
Jane Fitz-Randolph ; illustrated by Bruce Hiscock and with photographs.
p. cm.
Includes bibliographical references (p. 89) and index.
ISBN 0-689-31848-0
1. Archaeological dating—Juvenile literature. I. Fitz-Randolph, Jane. II. Hiscock, Bruce, ill. III. Title.
CC78.J47   1996   96-5170
930.1'028'5—dc20   CIP
AC

CONTENTS

Chapter 1

MYSTERIES EVERYWHERE

A trail of dinosaur tracks in her own backyard was nothing special to Betty Jo Ridennoure. Ever since she could remember, her father and other ranchers had talked about the giant footprints that started at the edge of the Purgatoire River in southeastern Colorado and ambled away from the shallow water toward higher ground. As a curiosity, Betty Jo's father had set up near the gatepost of the family home a stone slab that bore one of the huge footprints. Some of the older boys who spent spare time exploring caves in the canyons that branched off from the river had seen the trail of tracks. But they were more interested in things like the Spanish helmet and breastplate of chain mesh—probably from the days when Coronado and his men passed through the area—than in dinosaur tracks. The tracks were eleven miles from Betty Jo's home. There was only a rough ranch road, and the rugged terrain was covered with prickly cactus. Rattlesnakes and scorpions slithered and scurried over the ground. Always the same, the dinosaur tracks had been there for millions of years and would be there for millions more. So visits to look at them were rare.

Then one fall day in 1935, when Betty Jo was thirteen and a freshman at La Junta High School, she told her science teacher, Donald Hayes, about the dinosaur trail. Fascinated, he soon planned an expedition with a friend and Betty Jo to go and see the place.

They found two kinds of tracks. One looked like the imprint of a giant turkey, with three long toes. The other was like an elephant's foot, almost round, with short stubby toes. Each print was like a shallow basin about three inches deep, eleven inches wide, and fifteen inches long. Eighteen of them, about forty-eight inches apart, formed an almost straight line. The trail disappeared when it reached a bank, where there were probably more tracks covered by several feet of hard soil. Millions of years ago, Mr. Hayes explained, the dinosaurs had walked along what must have been the muddy shore of a shrinking lake. The mud had dried very slowly and hardened into stone.

Mr. Hayes wrote to experts in the eastern United States, who came to see the tracks. They identified the birdlike tracks as those of an allosaurus and the large round ones as those of the huge brontosaurus, which weighed about thirty-three tons. One of the scientists said he thought the trail was probably the longest known in the world, which it has proved to be. Much later, when scientists removed soil from the ancient rock base, they found that not just one, but *five* brontosauruses had walked along the lakeshore side by side! Today the area is under the protection of the National Park Service.

Five years after Betty Jo's expedition with her teacher, in 1940, a French boy from the village of Montignac, in southwestern France, noticed an odd-looking hole in the ground next to a newly uprooted pine tree. After tossing a few stones into the hole to test its depth, he and a few friends dug the hole a little bigger and saw that it was the mouth of a steeply sloping tunnel. They got a flashlight and started to explore. Slipping and sliding

In 1940, schoolboys discovered hundreds of drawings and engravings made seventeen thousand years ago on the walls of a huge cave in France. LASCAUX CAVE

on the wet clay, they landed in a dark cave much deeper than they had expected. The cave was huge. Shining their light around, they were amazed to find the walls covered with paintings of large animals—bulls. Some were more than fifteen feet long.

Looking for an easier way out than climbing up the slippery clay, the boys found passages that led to other large rooms. Here too the walls and ceilings were covered with paintings of various animals.

Finally the boys had to retrace their steps; and when they came out into the light of day, they discussed what they should do about their discovery. They knew they would be scolded, probably punished, for foolishly

entering a dangerous tunnel. Probably nobody would believe their fantas-
tic story. But they had to tell *somebody* about their strange findings.

In the end, they told their schoolmaster, and persuaded him to go with
them to see the animal paintings for himself. The story was printed in the
school paper, and the schoolmaster told a professional archaeologist, Abbe
Henri Breuil, about the find. Soon other experts in prehistoric studies came
to see the incredible paintings.

The boys had discovered what came to be known as the Lascaux Cave,
for some twenty years a main tourist attraction in France. (When the artwork began to show damage simply from exposure to the large numbers of
sightseers walking through the cave, scientists decided to close it to all but
persons with some special reason for being there. At great expense, the
government opened another cave nearby, where artists made paintings like
those in the original cave for tourists to look at.) The scientists counted
more than 1,500 engravings and drawings, along with lamps, painting tools,
and other artifacts. They said the work was done during the Old Stone
Age, seventeen thousand years ago.

How do scientists go about finding out the history of mysterious old
objects? How can they tell how old things are—paintings on a cave wall,
an old bottle from a dump, fossils buried deep in beds of clay? How do they
know how old the earth is?

They begin by doing just what you would do. They collect all the facts
they can observe firsthand, being very careful not to destroy anything.
Before they move anything, they take pictures, make drawings and measurements, and write down many details. They label things, and keep
records of everything they do.

Then they start looking for clues that surround the object—rocks, wood,
cloth, dishes, tools, trash. Trash piles can be rich sources for clues. Some
clues are better than others. As in mystery stories, some clues that seem

most important and promising fade away or lead on a wild goose chase. Some bits of evidence that seem most vital prove to be nothing at all. And something that seemed hardly worth noting may be the key that unlocks the whole mystery.

At first the scientists' methods were crude, and so were their results. They could be fairly sure that a copper tool was probably older than a similar bronze tool found in the same area, because adding tin to copper to make a harder metal, bronze, showed an advancement in metal making. But about the best that scientists could say for very ancient objects found in a trash pile was that this object was probably older than that one because it was buried deeper in the pile. Presumably the oldest discards were covered by newer ones as the pile grew.

The scientists estimated the age of things within a few thousand or a few million years. A period that began in Europe about 3500 B.C. they called the Bronze Age, and placed tools and other objects made of bronze in this period. Before this was the Stone Age, when tools and weapons were made of stone. Often the scientists' estimates of age had to be changed. There were all kinds of contradictions, and "facts" that didn't fit together. Scientists disagreed on which and who was right. There were many unanswered questions, few with positive answers.

But as more and more professional and amateur scientists made more and more discoveries and pieced together more and more bits of information from all over the world, the great jigsaw puzzle of the past began to fill in. New and better tools and methods of investigation helped *archaeologists*, scientists who study remains from the past, to peg definite ages to things. There are still contradictions and disagreements, puzzles that only grow more puzzling. Findings thought to be accurate just a few years ago have had to be revised. Almost every day, scientists and amateurs poking around in familiar or unfamiliar places make new discoveries that either disprove theories or help to strengthen them. Sometimes explorers have a pretty good idea of where to poke. Other times they just stumble onto something.

New tools have expanded investigations and made the results more certain. Very powerful electron microscopes and other instruments developed in the last five to ten years give scientists ways to study the almost invisible fossils of spores and pollen from ancient trees and plants. CAT scans, which use X-ray machines aided by computers, let them look inside mummies without cutting into them. Molecular biologists find that a speck of blood from an arrow tip thousands of years old can tell them many things about the animal or human being struck by the arrow. Pictures made from satellites using infrared photography show man-made roads, canals, and buried cities that can be seen in no other way.

In this book we shall explore the many ways of finding the age of objects ranging from the relatively young—like pottery and old musical instruments—to fossils and the earth itself. We shall see that knowing the age of these objects is important because they are often markers that help us tie together events that happened thousands and millions of years ago. We shall see that some discoveries that seemed useless at first have proved to be important in locating ore deposits, understanding and predicting climate, and dealing with some of the problems of today's ecology and environment.

Chapter 2

REAL TEETH AND FAKE ART

If we want to know how old a horse is, we can just open his mouth and look at his teeth. The front teeth have little cups in the biting surfaces. As the horse grows older, the teeth gradually wear down, and the cups slowly disappear, in a known order and at certain ages. By the time the horse is nine or ten years old, his teeth are all worn smooth. When someone says that a piece of information is "straight from the horse's mouth," he means the truth of the information can't be disputed.

Finding the age of something is seldom this easy, and the results are often less definite, but scientists have found clever ways to solve even very difficult puzzles. Objects closest to the present time are usually easiest to date. Information sources are plentiful. Besides history books there are all kinds of other records. Grandparents and other relatives and friends know the history of family possessions. Museums have collections of everything from early airplanes and old farm machinery to antique military uniforms, glassware, and marbles. Scientists in charge of these places, called curators, know a great deal about the objects displayed there. So do hobbyists who collect and learn the history of vintage cars, model trains, old dolls, and hundreds of other things. Most are eager to share their knowledge and help identify and find the age of items on which they are experts.

Libraries have books with pictures and descriptions of antique jewelry, dishes, furniture, and almost anything else one can think of. Anyone who wishes to find out the age and history of some particular object from the last six or eight hundred years, and who is willing to give a little time and effort to some detective work, can generally find answers.

Having two or more different sources that agree makes the answer more likely to be right. If Uncle Hank says his cherished twenty-one-jewel railroad watch that his father gave him was made in 1921—and the local jeweler has a catalog with a picture and description of the watch, and it says these watches were made from 1921 to 1924—then Uncle Hank's account is probably true.

But sometimes even the experts miss. In 1974 the Cleveland (Ohio) Museum of Art paid a million dollars for a painting of St. Catherine by a sixteenth-century artist, Matthias Gruenwald. An art history expert had doubts about the painting and asked a German art authority, Robert von Sonnenburg, to examine it. Using an electron microscope, an X-ray machine, and some chemical tests, von Sonnenburg found several bits of evidence that showed the painting was a fake. A basic ingredient of the paint was a processed chalk that did not exist when the painter lived, four hundred years ago. And although silver was always a part of white lead paint until well into the 1800s, there was no silver in the paint he tested.

The fake painting turned out to be the work of a Bavarian artist who restores old paintings. He is proud of the paintings he makes in the style of old masters. He is even proud of his ability to "age" his paintings several hundred years in less than one day, a process that ends with smearing dirt on them.

There are many stories of art fakes that have fooled the experts. A violin found in an old attic trunk and marked "Stradivarius," or with another famous maker's name, is almost certainly an imitation. Manuscripts and letters supposedly written by famous people, and even bearing their forged signatures, turn up from time to time. Copies of old jewelry, glass, and other objects are sometimes so well done that they are hard to be sure about. But today's experts have examined enough samples in their field, and have learned enough about the history of their specialty, to have a pretty good hunch about a piece they are studying. And tests with high-powered microscopes, spectrometers, and other recently developed instruments and methods help them make dependable evaluations.

• • •

Columbus's records of his first trip to the New World five hundred years ago tell of the grounding of his flagship, the *Santa María*, on a coral reef off the north coast of the Caribbean island that now contains Haiti and the Dominican Republic. It was Christmas Eve, 1492. The ship was damaged beyond repair; and the next day, with help from local natives and their canoes, the crew moved supplies ashore, along with pieces of the dismantled ship. The native chieftain gave them a site with two houses on it, where Columbus and his men set up a small settlement that they named La Navidad, Spanish for "the nativity," to celebrate the Christmas date of their safe landing.

Leaving thirty-nine men there with orders to build a fort and to trade with the natives for as much gold as they could get before he returned, Columbus and his other men set sail in the two remaining ships, the *Niña* and the *Pinta*. But when he came back a year later, La Navidad had been burned and all his men were dead.

No one made any serious efforts to locate the site of La Navidad until a small team of scientists from the Florida State Museum began exploring a place discovered in 1977 by an amateur archaeologist, Dr. William Hodges. Hodges had been interested in several sites in the area that looked like possible abandoned settlements. The scientists spent parts of three years digging into a raised mound in what they thought was the central plaza of an old settlement that could be La Navidad.

Careful sifting of trash from the pit produced a pig's tooth and the jawbone of a rat—animals unknown in the New World before Columbus. COURTESY FLORIDA MUSEUM OF NATURAL HISTORY

Here they found a filled-in pit seven feet deep and a yard across. The pit, they believed, could have been a well; and since wells were not known in the Caribbean native culture, its very existence suggested that it had been dug and used by Europeans. In the well they found charred wood, bones, and bits of pottery and glass. *Carbon 14 dating* and *thermoluminescence* tests—two dating methods we shall discuss later—showed that the charcoal came from fires within thirty-five years before or after 1440. This, of course, was too early for Columbus, although it comes fairly close.

But then other scientists, directed by Dr. Elizabeth Wing of the Florida State Museum, made more discoveries. Deep in the pit they found the jawbone of a rat and the tooth of a pig. Neither of these animals was known in the New World before Columbus. So this seemed to be reliable proof that the pit had been filled in after 1492.

Later another scientist, Dr. Jonathan Ericson at the University of California at Irvine, analyzed strontium atoms in the pig's tooth. Teeth are very durable, and they often play an important part in establishing a date. As an animal grows, its developing teeth take on chemical elements found in its diet. Plants grown in a soil that contains certain chemicals absorb some of these chemicals. Then the flesh and bones and teeth of animals that eat the plants absorb the chemicals from the plants. Dr. Ericson's studies showed that the pig had probably lived in Seville, in Spain, close to Palos, the port from which Columbus sailed. The soil in this area is very rich in strontium.

The search continues for more pieces of the puzzle, but the scientists feel sure they have found what is left of La Navidad, the first Spanish settlement in the New World.

Chapter 3

FROM POTSHERDS TO CARBON ATOMS

August 24, A.D. 79. The date was never in question, as hundreds of people from nearby towns rushed to rescue survivors of the violent explosion of Mount Vesuvius. The eruption had buried the ancient Italian city of Pompeii almost instantly under twenty feet of cinders and fine white ashes. There were no rivers of red-hot lava such as we often associate with volcanoes—just the much cooler dry ashes that covered everything like a thick blanket.

When archaeologists began excavating the ruin nearly 1,600 years later, they were astounded to find that almost nothing had been destroyed. Many residents had heeded the warning signs of earthquakes and small emissions from the volcano and had fled, taking their most prized possessions with them. But the activities of those who had stayed behind were frozen in a moment of time. Skeletons of victims lay in the streets, in shops and homes. Dishes, eating utensils, loaves of bread, and glass bowls of beans and fruit were still on the tables. Shops held common tools of blacksmiths and silversmiths. Fishing nets and boating gear hung on the painted walls.

Pompeii became famous throughout the world as silver vases, marble statues, and other artifacts from the ancient city were displayed in museums of Europe and elsewhere.

Today visitors to Pompeii see many of these objects furnishing the excavated houses and buildings, just as they must have looked before the volcano struck. In other places, tombs of kings are valued for their carefully prepared mummies and wealth of jewels, precious metals, and special objects buried with the dead. But because it showed the everyday life and activities of common people, Pompeii was considered unique in all the world.

Then in 1976, half a world away in El Salvador, in Central America, a man lowering a hillside with a bulldozer unexpectedly struck something large and solid. Buried in fine black volcanic ash was a very well preserved adobe house. Bulldozing ceased while experts were called in to see what had been unearthed.

Because the house was in such good condition, officials from El Salvador's National Museum thought it was a recent building of little interest. Two years passed before the first archaeologist visited the site. Dr. Payson Sheets, from the University of Colorado, had dug in other sites in the area, and he, too, thought the ruin—known now as Ceren—was recent. Curious observers reported seeing remains of a human family huddled on the floor of the house, but by the time Dr. Sheets arrived all such evidence had been bulldozed away.

As Sheets sifted through ashes in the house, he expected to find pieces of metal, glass, or plastic. Instead, he was amazed to find bits of colorful pottery that he recognized as common in that part of Central America from about A.D. 300 to 900. Pottery is always an important clue to establish the age of things found with it. A basic need of people everywhere and throughout time is for plates and bowls and jugs for storing, cooking, and serving food. Clay is a useful and plentiful sub-stance from which to shape containers; and made into pottery, it is very durable. So broken bits of pottery—and sometimes whole pieces—are abundant almost everywhere that people have lived.

Stone pillars resting on stone steps mark the doorway of the first building unearthed at Ceren, now called Household 1. The stone bench just inside was probably used for sleeping and daytime family activities.
COURTESY PAYSON SHEETS

By studying pottery from different times and places all over the world, scientists have learned to tell a great deal about the pieces that turn up almost anywhere. Clays found in different places have different textures and colors; they contain different minerals and other substances. Different groups of people had their own way to shape the pieces they made, different designs, decorations and colors. They had different ways to harden and polish the clay. So much has been written and pictured of pottery from all parts of the world that experts readily recognize even broken bits—called potsherds or simply sherds—and can tell when and where they were made.

Just digging at random in a promising site with the hope of bumping into something worthwhile is very costly and time consuming. Big machines can easily destroy the most precious treasure. The more archaeologists can find out about their "dig" before breaking ground, the better. Fortunately they have found some ingenious ways to use modern technology to help them. For example, a special radar instrument, moved back and forth across an area, can tell them the location, size, and sometimes the kind of anomalies—unnatural objects such as walls or buildings—buried as much as twenty-five feet below the surface. Although this is not actually a part of finding out how old something is, scientists have to find the box and open it before they can study what's inside.

In Ceren, Sheets and his fellow scientists and students spent several summers excavating the adobe house and the space around it. Besides sherds they found stone tools and ceramic artwork. They also found woven mats, pots full of beans, and fields of planted corn with mature ears. This led them to believe that the area had been buried by ashes from a volcano that had probably erupted in August. They sent samples of the thatched roof of the house and other organic materials to the University of Texas for carbon dating. Results showed that the ashes had buried the site about A.D. 600.

An architect's drawing of Household 1 shows the front steps and doorway, along with two outbuildings as they must have looked before the volcano buried them. COURTESY PAYSON SHEETS

What is carbon dating, and how does it work? Carbon dating—also called carbon 14 or sometimes radiocarbon dating—is a reliable and now common method pioneered by Dr. William F. Libby of the University of Chicago. Its purpose is to find the age of anything that was once alive. Carbon dating works with specimens that were alive up to about fifty thousand years ago. A number of similar tests have been developed for dating different kinds of things, but because carbon dating was the first and is still one of the most used, we'll leave Ceren for a bit while we discuss this method.

The smallest chunk of every element in the universe is its *atom*. All atoms are made of different numbers and arrangements of three basic building blocks—*protons* and *neutrons* in the atom's nucleus, and *electrons* that rotate around the nucleus like planets around our sun. It is the differences in the numbers and arrangements of these building blocks that make gold, gold, and oxygen, oxygen.

Most atoms are "stable." That is, an atom of gold will remain gold forever. Some elements have a normal, stable atom and also an *un*stable atom. Unstable atoms change or "decay" into some other, stable element. And because they give off radiation as they decay, they are "radioactive."

Carbon has a stable atom, which is carbon 12. Carbon 12 has six protons and six neutrons in its nucleus. Carbon also has an unstable, radioactive atom, which has two extra neutrons—six protons and eight neutrons—in its nucleus, so it is *carbon 14*. The number of protons in the nucleus determines what kind of atom it is. Hydrogen has one proton in its nucleus, carbon has six, and nitrogen, seven. Atoms with the same number of protons in their nuclei but different numbers of neutrons are called *isotopes* of that element; carbon 14 is an isotope of the element carbon.

As a carbon 14 atom decays, one of the neutrons turns into a proton, and it becomes a *nitrogen* atom, a stable (nonradioactive) atom of the element nitrogen. (See Figure 1.) This decay process follows a very definite

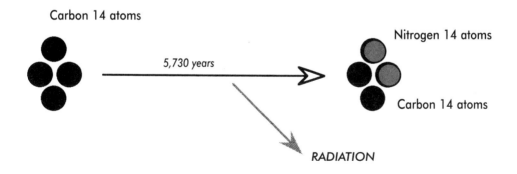

FIGURE 1. *Some of the unstable carbon 14 atoms become nitrogen atoms.*

and predictable schedule. Whether the atoms are carbon 14 or atoms of some other element, it always takes a specific amount of time for half of the atoms to decay. That is, at the end of a certain predictable time, half of the atoms will have decayed. Scientists use the term *half-life* to describe this process. The half-life of carbon 14 is 5,730 years. That is, no matter how many carbon 14 atoms we start out with, it takes 5,730 years for half of them to turn into nitrogen atoms. Experiments show that the half-life is not affected by changes in temperature, pressure, or humidity.

What has all of this to do with finding out how old something is? Well, in a series of physical and chemical processes in nature, carbon 14 is constantly being created in earth's atmosphere, all over the world. The carbon 14 and carbon 12 atoms combine with oxygen atoms in the atmosphere to make the common gas carbon dioxide.

In a process called photosynthesis, trees, shrubs, and all living plants absorb carbon dioxide from the air. So all living plants have very small amounts of carbon 14 throughout their tissues. Since people and all animals eat fruits, vegetables, and leafy plants, they too have carbon 14 in their bodies. So all living things contain carbon 14.

But as soon as a plant or animal or human being dies, the intake of carbon 14 ceases, and the radioactive carbon 14 atoms in the body start to decay into nitrogen. So the number of carbon 14 atoms slowly decreases while the number of stable carbon 12 atoms remains the same. Since the half-life of carbon 14 is 5,730 years, we know that at the end of this time there will be half as much carbon 14 as there was at the end of the first 5,730 years—and so on, as time progresses. This is the way the half-life principle works. (See Figure 2.)

Now we see how carbon 14 is the key to knowing the age of anything that was once alive. Using a table that shows the amount of carbon 14 compared to carbon 12 in a sample they are testing, scientists can tell its age to within thirty to fifty years, back to fifty thousand years ago. With today's measuring techniques, less than one-thousandth of an ounce of material is enough to test for age. Scientists can find the age of things as tiny as tree pollens and one-cell animals. The carbon 14 test is the most widely used method for dating ancient plants and animals.

When Payson Sheets and his team returned to Ceren in the spring of 1989, a geophysicist who was part of the team used a *resistivity* instrument to locate other buildings. This is a simple device that consists of two long steel rods connected to the two terminals of a big battery. When the

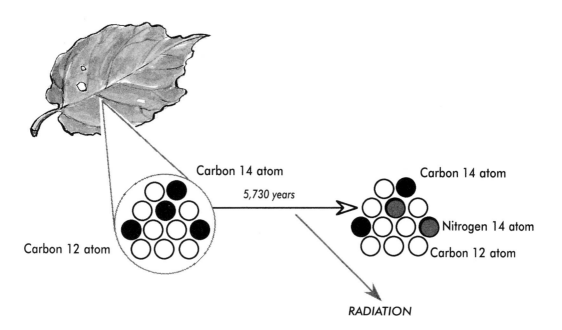

FIGURE 2. *After 5,730 years only half of the carbon 14 atoms will be left.*

rods are driven into the ground ten to fifteen feet apart, the ground between them acts as an electrical conductor. Dry, sandy ground—or dry volcanic ash—is a poor conductor. Wet ground is a good conductor, as is muddy, mineral-laden water that tends to collect in the bottom of a buried building or along a wall. A meter tells when the current is flowing through a good conductor. By moving one or both rods from place to place and recording the resistance—or conductivity—shown by the meter, scientists can plot a map of what is probably buried beneath the ground. (See Figure 3.)

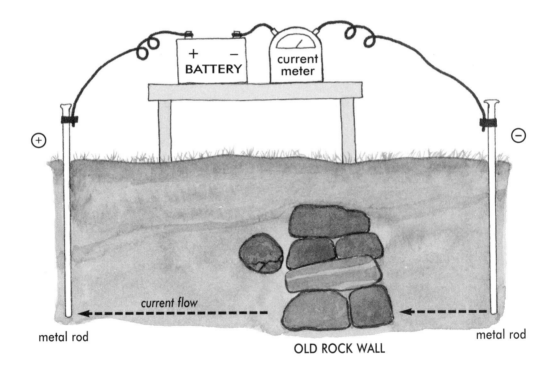

FIGURE 3. *A meter shows how much current is flowing through the ground. This helps to locate buried walls or other objects.*

A core drilling rig brings up samples of everything the drill passes through.
COURTESY PAYSON SHEETS

Before starting to dig where the buildings seemed likely to be, Sheets brought in a group of Salvadoran technicians to get core samples that would show what he might find. In this process, a hollow drill bores straight down, collecting a cylinder of earth that contains samples of everything the drill passes through. (See Figure 4.)

That summer the team unearthed two more buildings and found many artifacts that helped piece together the culture and activities of the people who had lived there 1,400 years ago. Bowls and decorative pieces of ceramic art had been tucked away in many nooks and niches in the adobe walls. One house held many pottery vessels, grinding stones, and cutting tools made of obsidian, a glossy volcanic rock. All obsidian blades with sharp cutting edges had been carefully secured up in the roofing thatch, probably, Sheets says, to protect the edges from damage, but also to keep them out of reach of children who might cut themselves. An especially interesting find was a bowl turned upside down and put away—apparently in haste—in one of the niches. The bowl still held a thin film of food, and the marks of three fingers swiped through the food

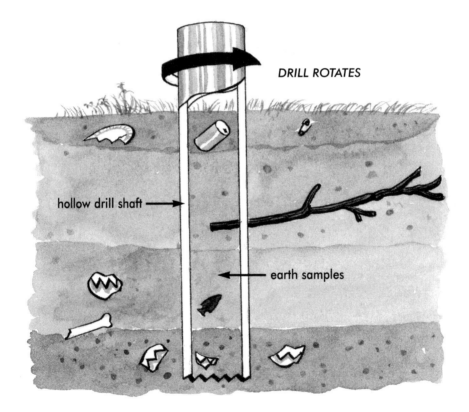

FIGURE 4. *As the drill penetrates the Earth, it collects a core sample.*

Special radar equipment can locate buildings and other solid objects one to twenty feet underground. When electrical "noise" from their Jeep's motor spoiled information gathered by the highly sensitive electronic instruments, the scientists loaded their instruments into a cart pulled by a patient ox. COURTESY PAYSON SHEETS

and up the side of the bowl by someone eating in a way common to many cultures even today.

The excavation of Ceren has only begun. No human remains have yet been found, but the scientists know from their radar and other probes that many more buildings are buried under the volcanic ash; some of them doubtless contain skeletons of human beings. As in Pompeii, the excavation work will go on for many years—perhaps lifetimes, Sheets says. Although the artifacts found in Ceren are from a primitive culture, not an advanced civilization like that of Pompeii, both resulted from the sudden smothering of a people going about their daily activities; so Ceren is often referred to as the Pompeii of the western hemisphere.

Chapter 4

CALENDARS IN TREES

On May 19, 1980, another volcano, Mount St. Helens, in the state of Washington, blew off a great chunk of its mountainside. Light gray ash sifted over large expanses of the western United States. Like the eruption of Mount Vesuvius in 79, the date was never in doubt. Scientists had predicted it weeks, days, then hours before it happened. Viewers all over the world saw it on TV.

Mount St. Helens had erupted before, in 1480 and again in 1482. That was more than five hundred years ago, before Columbus had visited the New World. Who was present to make a note of these events? How had they been recorded and preserved?

To answer these questions we need to look at a way of pinpointing dates more precisely than is possible with carbon 14 dating. We have seen how trees play two roles in carbon dating. First, along with other leafy plants, they absorb carbon dioxide from the air and start the chain of chemical action that results in carbon atoms in every living thing. Second, charcoal from burned wood or wood used to build things thousands of years ago can supply material to test with carbon dating. But trees also provide another, totally different way to find the age of things and tell us when and where events took place.

Tree-ring dating is a fairly new method for studying when something happened. The stump of a tree that was recently cut down—or the sawed end of the tree—shows light and dark rings that circle a dark spot in the center like rings of a target around the bull's-eye. The rings form as the tree grows; each ring represents one year of the tree's life.

Although they look almost alike, there are important differences in the rings. During years of heavy rainfall, the cells of a growing tree are larger and less dense than in dry years. The rings for wet years with a long growing season are thicker than those for dry, cold years, and spaces between rings are wider. Each ring tells something about what happened in the area that year, and together the rings provide a record of events in the tree's life. Tree-ring study, or *dendrochronology*, tells scientists much more than just how old a certain tree is, although it can do this very precisely.

Scientific studies have shown that numbers of samples from the same area have matching ring patterns. One scientist, David Yamaguchi of the University of Colorado, says the ring patterns are like the bar codes on products at a grocery store. Scientists experienced in reading the codes have a very clear idea of floods, fires, droughts, and climate changes in areas where the trees grew.

Studying samples from trees near Mount St. Helens volcano, Yamaguchi found evidence of the major eruptions that had taken place in 1480 and 1482. The lower parts of the trunks of some trees that grew in the area where nearly everything was killed by the volcano were buried in several feet of ashes. Yamaguchi compared the ring patterns of these trees with those of trees growing outside the ash-covered area. He found that in the

Although much of the tree is dead, core drillings that include still-living bark show this Colorado bristlecone pine to be more than 2,400 years old.
COURTESY UNIVERSITY OF COLORADO, BOULDER. PHOTO BY KEN ABBOTT.

trees that had survived the volcanoes, the rings for those two years were often missing because the stress had prevented growth. Further research showed two more major eruptions in 1800. Findings like these help scientists who study volcanoes predict when further eruptions may occur.

Yamaguchi also made a study of tree-ring samples from a sixty-mile stretch of Washington State's southern coastline. Here he found that about three hundred years ago, scores of healthy cedar trees had died suddenly and all at the same time. Comparing ring patterns of these trees with those of other trees in the area that had survived longer showed that a superlarge earthquake had happened there at that time. Geologists and earthquake experts welcome such reports; the evidence helps them by adding to the facts from their own studies.

Of course, getting useful information of this kind from tree-ring analysis depends on having a reliable date from which to start counting. In the case of a living tree or one recently cut down, the outside ring, just under the bark is year one, the present year. Counting back from this one, a researcher can identify any year before the present. But how can a scientist know that a dead tree died three hundred years ago?

The simplest answer is to find a *living* tree that was growing in the same area at the time the dead tree died. Dr. Andrew Douglass, who founded the world-famous Laboratory of Tree-Ring Research at the University of Arizona in 1937, is considered the father of tree-ring science. Among the many things Douglass discovered was that ring patterns of a tree from a certain area can be matched perfectly with ring patterns of other trees from the same area, either living or dead. For example, a series of rings from a log used long ago to build a cabin may match a series from a living tree still growing in the same area. By matching the two patterns, and then count-ing the number of rings, or years, that the living tree has lived beyond the last ring of the old log, a scientist can tell when the log tree was cut down— and so judge how old the cabin is. (See Figure 1.) Using the same princi-ple, scientists can tell when a dead tree or many trees in the area died. Douglass called his technique *cross dating*. Working with archaeologists, he matched samples from living trees with samples cut from beams of old American Indian ruins in the southwestern United States. His cross-dating method helped to establish the age of more than six hundred ruins.

Counting the rings of a five-hundred-year-old tree—or even one that's only one hundred or sixty years old—is a chore. But dyes, microscopes, computers, and other modern tools make the task easier. Although a whole cross section of a tree is often most satisfactory to work with, it is not necessary to cut down a tree or remove a beam from a building to study the rings. Instead, scientists use a hollow drill to cut a core sample, often no thicker than a pencil, that shows a cross section of the tree or beam from its outside to its center—like those shown in the figure. They label their

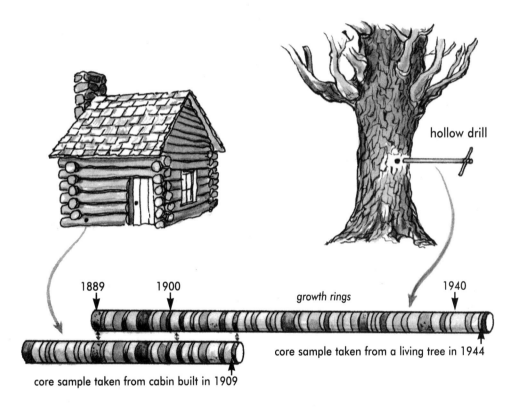

hollow drill

1889   1900   *growth rings*   1940

core sample taken from a living tree in 1944

core sample taken from cabin built in 1909

FIGURE 1. *Matching a sample from dead wood with one from a living tree gives a key to the age of the dead wood.*

core samples and sand them smooth. Then they can compare them with one another for cross dating and make a master series for a specific geographical area. With today's computer technology, they can examine many samples in great detail in just a short time.

Dendrochronologists have found that by matching sections of tree-ring patterns from older and older pieces of wood, they can put together a master series that may cover several thousand years. The big challenge in some areas is finding enough pieces of wood from trees whose lives overlapped

Rings from trees growing near Mount St. Helens show that the volcano had erupted in 1480 and 1482. COURTESY DAVID YAMAGUCHI

one another. More master series exist for parts of Europe and the British Isles than for the United States. Timbers from old sunken ships and Roman waterfront timbers have been dated back to A.D. 200 and even 100 B.C. There are also "floating" series in which patterns of two, three, or more wood samples match and overlap one another but at present have no tie to any known date. An Irish researcher hopes that as more scientists cross-date more and more samples, there may be an unbroken record of Europe that will go back 7,500 years. When used along with study of pottery pieces and other artifacts at a site, tree-ring dating can confirm the exact years when a site was occupied. It can also help to confirm and refine the results found by carbon dating.

How old is an "old" tree? The rings of the great sequoias and other majestic redwoods of California show that they were growing at the time of Christ. But some trees in the United States, much smaller and less spectacular, are twice that old. Some Great Basin bristlecone pine trees, found in California, Nevada, and Utah, are believed to be the world's oldest living trees. Tree-ring dating shows some are more than four thousand years old.

A Rocky Mountain bristlecone growing on a steep slope of loose rock in Colorado at an altitude of eleven thousand feet is believed to be Colorado's oldest living tree. It is thirty feet tall and four feet in diameter. Analysis of a core sample taken from it shows it to be 2,435 years old.

Bristlecones grow in extremely arid places, in poor rocky soil, often at altitudes of nine thousand feet and higher. Here the growing season is very short, and with fierce winter winds tearing constantly at their tops and branches, the trees grow very slowly. The rings are so fine and close together that scientists must use special dyes and high-powered micro-scopes to study and count the rings in the core samples they remove from the trees.

Today tree-ring scientists are studying their many samples to try to find out whether there is evidence that the climate of our planet is gradually growing warmer. Research has shown that the bristlecone pines are growing uncommonly fast in certain high-altitude areas. Some scientists think this may be due to increasing amounts of carbon dioxide in the air, which causes a "greenhouse effect" and holds warmth close to the earth. The whole study is very complex, but so far the general information from tree-ring study suggests that there have been many periods of warming and cooling throughout time, and the present time shows no real difference from previous warming times.

Tree-ring dating is still less than a hundred years old. But already it has been used for such widely different things as verifying the age of old violins and wood sculptures and carvings, and helping scientists understand the earth's climate hundreds of years ago. As tree-ring experts gather more and more samples from locations around the world, they will prepare more complete master series for each area. As pieces of the puzzle fill in, the scientists can supply more and more reliable information about environmental history. In the years ahead, they will be able to put together master series from more sources—possibly even from petrified trees from very ancient times. There are still many mysteries to unravel.

Chapter 5

LIBRARIES
IN CAVES

Kindergarten children are sometimes given a group of four or five pictures and asked to arrange them in a reasonable time sequence. One picture might show people picking apples, another a tree with fruit blossoms; a third could show a child eating a piece of apple pie, and the fourth a woman making the pie. Most children find the game fun and don't realize that it's developing important perception and reasoning processes.

One of the commonest and most obvious ways to find out when something happened or how old something is, is to find clues in the total situation that help establish a time frame. Let's suppose we find an old letter from a relative. The only date on it is "Tuesday," which is no help at all. But the letter includes a bit of information: "Uncle Louis has been so lonely since Aunt Clara died that I invited him to join us for Thanksgiving dinner. . . ." If we know when Aunt Clara died, then we can reason that the letter had to be written after her death but probably not very long after.

Similarly, the order in which things are buried in a trash heap or a cave is an important clue to the *relative* ages of things. Often we don't know the date, or *absolute* age of objects, but we know which were the oldest and which were younger. Unless there has been some big disturbance, such as a rooting around in the trash heap by curious but untrained explorers, the oldest objects will be near the bottom of the heap, the younger ones on top.

Primitive peoples everywhere were notoriously poor housekeepers. Their untidy habits are so predictable that one of the first things explorers or archaeologists look into is the trash pile that's almost certain to be just outside the entrance to the cave or house where the people lived. Or sometimes the trash heap itself may be all that's left to show where people had lived. In the heap are likely to be imperfect spear- or arrowheads, broken pottery, animal bones that may be dented or scratched by human teeth or a tool used to scrape off the meat—and sometimes a truly rare and unexpected treasure, such as the rat's jawbone mentioned in Chapter 2.

Almost always, the researchers and their helpers must spend weeks and months—often in isolated places with difficult working conditions—sifting through tons of sand and dirt to find anything worth saving. But once in a while something of great interest or value—such as drawings or paintings on a cave wall—is right out in plain sight.

What has been called "perhaps the most sensational archaeological event in our day" began in a cave in 1947. A goatherd from a nomadic Arab tribe called Bedouins was searching for a stray goat in a dry gulch in the desolate area northwest of the Dead Sea, in Palestine. He saw a cave in the rocks above him and tossed a stone into it to scare away any animal that might be there. To his great surprise, he heard a sound of shattering. Wondering what he could have hit, he got a friend to explore with him.

In the cave they found several large jars. One had been broken by the goatherd's stone. Hoping they had found a storehouse of coins, the two friends were disgusted when they discovered that the jars held only old rolls of leather and papyrus wrapped in cloth. They had smashed most of the jars and scattered some of the contents before it occurred to them that the rolls were old documents that someone might pay for. Gathering a few of the best, they set out to find a buyer.

What happened to the documents in the next several months is too complicated to tell here in detail. World War II had ended and the British government, which had governed the area since the end of World War I, announced that it was withdrawing. Jewish and Arab authorities in Palestine had more pressing matters to deal with than old manuscripts of unknown value. The merchants to whom the Bedouins tried to sell their loot showed little interest. So the manuscripts changed hands several times as they were smuggled from place to place before arriving at a monastery in Old Jerusalem. Here several local experts and others from France and Holland examined the manuscripts. The whole story of their discovery sounded so unlikely that almost no one believed it. One respected authority said flatly that no manuscript as old as these were said to be could have survived to this time. Most experts thought the manuscripts were frauds; some had been fooled before by such forgeries, which were common, and they did not wish to risk being fooled again.

The writing was dim, and the documents so brittle that they could be examined properly only in a well-equipped laboratory. But from what they could see, a few scholars believed them to be genuine copies of parts of the Bible, possibly almost as old as the original manuscripts. Most notable, and in better condition than the other documents, was a complete copy of the Book of Isaiah, from the Old Testament. Written in Hebrew, it consisted of seventeen sheets of leather sewn together to make a scroll nearly twenty-three feet long.

As stories of the manuscripts from the cave spread, specialists from Europe and the United States wanted to see what were becoming known as the Dead Sea Scrolls. Newspapers, magazines, and scientific journals

10 CM

Fragments of the Dead Sea Scrolls are so fragile that even the gentlest handling could destroy them. COURTESY ISRAEL ANTIQUITIES AUTHORITY

carried stories. Many still thought the documents were hoaxes and forgeries, but others were sure the writings were genuine.

The only way to be certain, they decided, was to visit the cave where the scrolls were found, and see what other artifacts they might collect there. But by this time authorities from various Palestinian government and religious groups were claiming ownership of the scrolls and wanted them returned. Delicate negotiations took time, and when the scientists finally got permission to inspect the cave, no one was sure just where it was. The area had many caves, and searchers had found many more manuscripts and artifacts in some of them.

When the scientists finally found the cave they were looking for, they discovered that other searchers had been there before them. Nothing remained but tiny fragments of pottery and bits of cloth, leather, and papyrus ground into the dirt on the floor of the cave. The scientists painstakingly collected some six hundred small scraps. From these they were able to recognize bits from three more books from the Old Testament. The pottery bits proved to be from the Greco-Roman period, 30 B.C. to A.D. 70.

Scholars and archaeologists from all over the world began to show interest in the findings. The Bedouin tribesmen found a ready market for the hundreds of jars, bowls, lamps, jugs, old coins—and more and more ancient manuscripts—they found in other caves in the area. Specialists from different countries, with different expertise, studied pottery sherds. They pieced together fragments of broken jars to see their size and shape. In an unbroken jar they found a coin that experts said positively was minted in A.D. 10. Using their knowledge of patterns, materials, and styles, the pottery experts dated Greek jars from the first century B.C. and Roman jars from the third century A.D.

Although some of the manuscripts were biblical, many were copies of other religious works of the period, laws, accounts of battles, and just records of taxes and business transactions. Languages included Hebrew, Greek, Aramaic, and Latin. Identifying and translating the writings was obviously going to be an almost endless task.

Some of the manuscripts were brought to the United States in the summer of 1949 to be examined by experts at the Oriental Institute of Chicago. The experts got into a violent dispute about the age and authenticity of the documents. To settle the dispute, they agreed to have the material tested by Professor Willard F. Libby, next door at the Chicago Institute of Nuclear Physics.

Libby had just begun using the carbon 14 method he had invented for dating organic materials. At that time it took a chunk of material as big as a walnut to do the tests. Unwilling to destroy even a small bit of the manuscript, Libby took bits of the linen in which the Isaiah manuscript had been wrapped, burned them to ashes, and counted the number of atoms of carbon 14 in the ashes with a Geiger counter, a device used by prospectors to find radioactive minerals. Tests showed that the flax plants from which the linen was made had been harvested during the first century A.D. The scroll wrapped in the linen certainly had to be older than the linen. It turned out that the scroll was written about 100 B.C.—at least six hundred years earlier than the earliest known Hebrew copy of Isaiah.

Explorations of other caves in the Dead Sea area continued through the 1950s and added to the incredible collection of artifacts and manuscripts already found. One cave, or group of caves, about eleven miles from the one discovered by the goatherd is of interest here because it had five distinct sections that showed five periods of human habitation, beginning about 4500 B.C.

In the top section, the excavators found sherds of Arab pottery and a few metal pieces they recognized as Arabic. Other explorers had apparently removed everything of real interest. But in the section below this were many artifacts from the time of the Roman occupation of Palestine and surrounding areas. Coins bearing the words and symbols of the period showed their dates to be A.D. 132 to 135. Sherds with Greek and Hebrew letters, wood and metal objects, and decaying remnants of leather and cloth were similar to items of the period collected elsewhere.

Two Greek literary works written on papyrus also came from this level. Most interesting of all were pieces of papyrus with messages written in Hebrew by Simon Bar Kokhba. These were addressed to Joshua ben Galgola, who was apparently in charge of a military post in the area. Bar

Kokhba was known to have been making guerrilla attacks from A.D. 132 to 135 against the Romans. His letters further established the date of this second most recent occupation of the caves.

There was a long period between this Roman occupation and the earlier occupation by Iron Age people who left their pieces of metal tools in the third section during the seventh and eighth centuries B.C. Below this section were metal tools and artwork from the Middle Bronze Age, which lasted from about 1700 to 1500 B.C. A beautifully carved green stone scarab, a stout beetle that had religious meaning to Egyptians from this period, was one of the interesting finds.

Flint tools and weapons appeared in the three lowest levels, but most commonly in the very bottom section. These were from the Late Stone Age, which ended in this area about 3500 B.C. The most interesting object from this section was a polished wood ax handle, fitted with leather thongs for attaching a flint blade.

Whole books have been written about the Dead Sea Scrolls, how their discovery led to the exploration of the many caves and collections of artifacts found there. Scientists continue to use newer and more precise methods for dating these things. Much is still to be learned about the scrolls' contents. So far, they have revealed nothing new or different from the accounts in the Bible; in fact, they show that the scribes who painstakingly made copies of the ancient writings were very faithful in reproducing them exactly.

From the Dead Sea Scrolls we shall go on to the uncovering of whole cities that disappeared from the face of the earth centuries ago.

Chapter 6

TREASURE HUNTING FROM OUTER SPACE

An old German folktale tells of a young man who wanders into a village inhabited by strange but charming people. The hero meets a beautiful girl, and they promptly fall in love. But then he discovers that the village is under a spell. Long ago it was totally buried in the earth, and it emerges every hundred years for only one day, during which life goes on just as it did at the time the village was buried.

Until about the middle of the nineteenth century, scholars and historians generally thought most of the stories in the Bible were simply fables and allegories set in mythical cities. These cities did not surface even for one day in a hundred years. They seemed never to have existed at all, and the people mentioned in the tales seemed to be mythical characters.

Then in 1843, Paul-Émile Botta, a French consul who was serving in Mesopotamia, the area between the Tigris and Euphrates Rivers in present-day Iraq, was curious about some strange-looking mounds on the banks of the Tigris. Besides being a consul, Botta was also an amateur anthropologist. With permission from the local government, he began digging in the mounds; and after a number of fruitless efforts at several locations, he made a discovery that led to some of the most important archaeological searches of all time. Much to his surprise, he uncovered a bas-relief sculpture of Assyrian king Sargon II, who conquered and plundered Israel from 720 to 710 B.C. Details of the battles are recorded in the Old Testament of the Bible, in the Second Book of Kings.

Botta also found what later proved to be the king's own accounts of his exploits, written in cuneiform, the strange, wedge-shaped letters that were the very beginning of writing. Details of the king's account and the biblical account were very much the same. King Sargon II was no myth.

This was only the beginning. Clay tablets and papyrus documents written in cuneiform began to appear from other sources. As scholars learned to read and translate the messages, more and more names of biblical characters, places, and events turned up in the writings.

In trying to fit together the pieces of "how old?" puzzles and understand the lives of ancient peoples, archaeologists usually have to begin with material artifacts found at a certain place. They look at pottery, tools and weapons, walls and buildings, sometimes mummies and skeletons. Using techniques such as those we've discussed, they date these objects to help get a picture of what life was like in the time and place where the things were found.

But in their study of the cities, people, and events mentioned in the Bible and other religious and historic writings, this usual process was reversed. The carefully recorded names of people and places had been preserved from the times when the people lived. Before writing was invented, family members faithfully memorized family lineage and passed this information to their children, who preserved it by telling it to *their* children. Eventually the stories were written down in documents that became the

Bible and other works, copied and recopied, and treasured by families and religious leaders.

With discoveries of bits of evidence that some biblical people, places, and events were real, excitement spread among archaeologists everywhere. Instead of trying to reconstruct a way of life from studying artifacts, they found themselves searching for artifacts to prove the biblical accounts. If some of these stories were true, who knew what others might be true?

Between 1869 and 1901, French, British, American, and German scholars and scientists established research institutes to study sites in the Middle East. Archaeologists began digging in Mesopotamia, long considered the "cradle of civilization," and in Palestine and Egypt. To their amazement, they found that many places referred to in the Bible were precisely where the biblical stories said they were, and that often they looked exactly the way the biblical stories described them. Eager researchers reported that they had located the city of Babel, site of the infamous tower built by descendants of one of Noah's sons. They found what they felt sure was the mountain fortress of King Saul, where David played his harp and sang his psalms to soothe the troubled ruler. They announced the discovery of the stables of King Solomon, who had "twelve thousand horsemen." And they found much more, including whole cities that had been buried under desert sands for thousands of years. Although some of their reports were later discredited, many of their findings proved to be true. Accounts in the Talmud, the Bible, the Koran, and other religious writings supply so many "markers" that scholars need only to translate these into our own familiar terms to know when and where events took place. What many had considered mythology was becoming history.

One lost city that archaeologists longed to find was the five-thousand-year-old fortress city of Ubar, described in the Koran as the "city of towers."

Ubar—if it existed at all—was thought to be in a desolate area of the Arabian Peninsula known as Rub' al Khali, the "Empty Quarter," in present-day Oman. The literary classic *A Thousand and One Arabian Nights* depicts Ubar as the rich center of the frankincense trade for thirty centuries. Frankincense was a valuable substance made from the gum of bushes that grow in the area. It was used for medicines and perfumes. Processed in Ubar, it was shipped to Sumer, Damascus, and Jerusalem. Surely Ubar must be an archaeological prize, but finding it in the trackless desert seemed so chancy that nobody was willing to put up money for the search. Archaeologists needed a better idea of where to dig.

Again new technologies offered hope. In the late 1970s, geologists had begun using techniques developed by the Jet Propulsion Laboratory (JPL), in California, to help locate likely oil fields and mineral deposits. A few archaeologists had experimented with the same techniques to explore sites in Greece and Central America. They found that sensors on a satellite or space shuttle 250 miles above the earth could create a picture that showed ground features they could see in no other way.

The scientists combine information from two kinds of sensors. The first beams radar waves back to earth. When the waves strike objects on the ground, they bounce back to a receiver on the satellite. The receiver provides a kind of picture of the ground surface. (See Figure 1.)

The second kind of sensor detects two kinds of radiation. One is simply sunlight reflected from objects on the ground; it's somewhat like a very sophisticated still or movie camera. The other kind of radiation is the heat of infrared waves radiated from the ground. This radiation is not due to reflected sunlight—at least not directly. What happens is that sunlight falling on an object heats it—as the summer sun heats the sidewalk so hot that we can't stand on it barefoot. The warmed object radiates infrared waves, and this radiation is picked up by the sensor on the satellite—or even on a balloon or airplane. Most amazingly and helpfully, this sensor can gather information from several feet below the surface soil, sand, or volcanic ash, to reveal roads, canals, walls, cemeteries, buildings, and other features that may have been buried for hundreds or thousands of years. (See Figure 2.) The situation is much like that of a large rock buried a few inches or a foot under the front lawn. The rock, even though it's buried, absorbs heat from the sun—often so much that grass won't grow well above it. We can't see the rock, but a sensor can.

Information from both kinds of sensors is recorded in a form that can be fed into a computer. The computer combines all the data and generates a color map of the territory—a map that shows both surface and below-the-

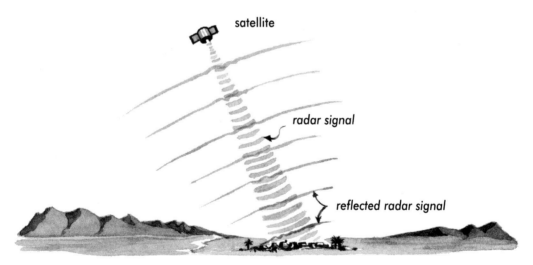

REMAINS OF AN ANCIENT CITY

Figure 1. Radar waves from satellite bounce back from objects on the ground.

surface details that no one could ever find by walking over or even survey-ing the ground.

With such a map in hand, geologists and engineers go to the area and inspect the land to see which colors match which surface features. This process is called *ground truthing*. It does not tell where a lost city or other target is, but it gives scientists a good idea of where to dig—or not to dig. It can save scientists years, even lifetimes, of fruitless digging and enormous amounts of money spent digging where there is nothing to find.

In 1984, Nicholas Clapp, a filmmaker with a longtime interest in Arabian history, asked Ronald Blom, a geologist at JPL, to help him find Ubar. JPL scientists developed a special combination of information for the

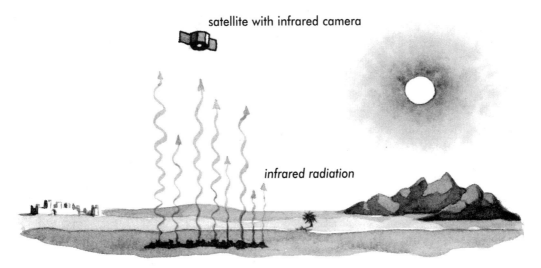

FIGURE 2. *An infrared sensor can detect objects buried underground.*

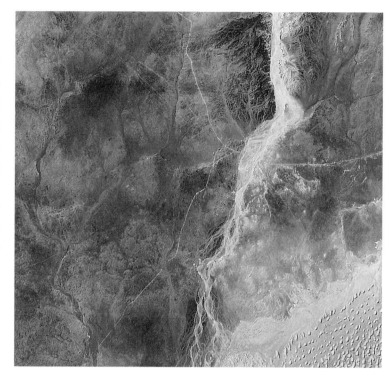

Electric sensors that "see" what is buried under surface soil revealed ancient roads that meet in a triangle. Researchers thought this a likely site for the lost city of Ubar.

COURTESY
JET PROPULSION
LABORATORY

project. They collected radar images taken in 1985 from the space shuttle *Challenger* and combined these with various images from some French-owned satellites and aerial photographs.

The upper left part of the map pictured here shows sand dunes in the Empty Quarter; it was a sandy yellow in the color photograph. A wadi, or dry riverbed, flows through the middle of the picture; it was blue in the color photo. The light-colored roads that run through the map form a tri-angle around the village called Shisr, thought at the time of the mapping to be the likely location of Ubar. These roads are very ancient.

In the summer of 1991, work crews did some exploratory digging at about thirty-five promising-looking sites in this area, but they found nothing. More study of the map made from outer space showed that the underground water tables where they had been digging would not have been large enough to provide water for a city the size of Ubar. An area farther east looked more promising, and the operation moved to that location.

By November, some forty diggers had found a fortress surrounded by eight walls, each about ten feet high and two feet thick. They also found pieces of Roman, Greek, and Syrian pottery. The exploration continues, although much of the city seems to have fallen into a hole in the limestone beneath it and expert engineering techniques will be needed to excavate it without causing further damage. Thermoluminescence dating of the pottery—a technique we shall discuss in detail in the next chapter—along with historical written accounts of Ubar and its trade, shows that this is almost certainly the city that was the frankincense trade center dating back to 3000 to 4000 B.C.

Smaller remote-sensing instruments suspended from an airplane or other aircraft, or even carried by a person walking over a site, can pick out specific areas to explore. Using such a hand-carried device, scientists exploring a site in Greece found a stone ax head and tools that dated from the Early Ice Age, two hundred thousand to five hundred thousand years ago. Their find is the earliest evidence of human life in Greece.

Chapter 7

MUMMIES AND SKELETONS

When someone mentions mummies, we think of long-dead human bodies tightly wrapped in bandagelike strips of cloth. Probably we also think of the famous Pyramids and other tombs near the Nile River, where the mummies of ancient Egyptian rulers were preserved, some of them for three thousand years. These tombs are basic information sources for Egyptologists, the scientists who specialize in the history of this area, and other scientists interested in ancient civilizations.

The very earliest mummies, some four thousand years old, were "natural" mummies. Bodies buried in the hot, dry desert sand simply dried up instead of decaying. Then as people's belief in the afterlife grew, early civilizations developed more elaborate ways of preserving bodies. Embalmers used new methods and chemicals, along with religious rituals that included placing jewels and amulets with the body. Often they also placed in the tomb various bowls and dishes, armor, and other objects that they assumed the dead person would need in the life to come.

Hieroglyphs, or picture writing, on the walls of tombs were a mystery until 1822, when a French scholar discovered the key to deciphering them. With this key, researchers were able to tell a great deal about just who was buried in the tomb, the family and age of the person, and something about the time in which he lived. This also helped to date the various objects buried with the person. More recently, carbon dating has also been used to establish the age of some mummies, and thus help to verify their identity.

Computers and modern medical technology can also help to find the age and many other details of ancient mummies. In 1990, several scientists at the University of Illinois in Urbana used their expertise in a year-long study of a mummy about which nothing at all was known. All that observers could see was the "packaging"—brown wrappings cemented and hardened by long-dried resins—that bore a few faded images of Egyptian gods. The bottom of the package was missing. Two gray stubs of leg bones showed that the feet had been broken off at the ankles. The wrappings and images were like those of other mummies known to be about two thousand years old. Curators at the university's World Heritage Museum, which had just acquired the mummy and planned to use it in a display, wanted to know what was inside the package, but they told the researchers that they could not open it or invade it to find out.

The scientists put the whole package into the CAT scanner at the university's Large Animal Clinic. The scanner is simply a capsule with a turntable inside for mounting the object to be studied. The operators make X-ray images of the object from many different angles. Then, using a computer, they combine these images to make three-dimensional images from any angle they wish. One scientist describes the result as being like a bowl of Jell-O salad in which a person can study the pieces of fruit embedded in different places and positions in the Jell-O.

The CAT scans showed some important facts about the mummy in the case. The ends of the long bones of the arms and legs were not yet fused.

These areas, where the bone growth takes place, show up darker in X rays of a growing young person than in the X rays of one whose bones are fully developed. Although the feet are missing, X-ray images of the knee development showed that the mummy was a preteen. When the anthropologist who studied the X rays looked at the mummy's jawbone from several angles, she noticed adult teeth coming in behind the baby teeth. This showed that the mummy was between seven and nine years old at the time of death.

Scientists generally place Egyptian mummies and artifacts in time by naming the *dynasty* in which they belong. This was a timescale or calendar used by the ancient Egyptians. Instead of measuring ongoing time as we do, dating events B.C. or A.D., they set their calendar back to zero each time a new bloodline of kings came to power. They had no way of knowing, of course, that they were living "B.C.," since such dates did not exist before the birth of Christ. By our timescale, the first dynasty lasted from 3400 to 3200 B.C. The most carefully preserved Egyptian mummies are from the Twenty-first and Twenty-second dynasties, from 1075 to 919 B.C.

Mummies have also been found in other parts of the world. Some natural mummies have come from hot, dry areas of the southwestern United States. But ancient civilizations in Venezuela, Ecuador, Colombia,

Museum staff members wanted to know about the mummy wrapped in this package, but they would not allow researchers to open or make a hole in it.
COURTESY WORLD HERITAGE MUSEUM, UNIVERSITY OF ILLINOIS

Bolivia, Peru, and elsewhere in South, Central, and North America prepared their dead for mummification in much the same way as the ancient Egyptians did. Similar procedures have also been observed in mummies found in the Canary Islands. Some mummy experts think Egyptian practices may somehow have spread over a very large part of the earth. Carbon dating helps scientists identify mummies from everywhere; their age is often an important key to knowing who they were.

In early 1992, some 225 mummy experts from twenty countries met for a week in the Canary Islands for the First World Congress on Mummy Studies. Mummy study, the scientists said, had for too long been seen more as a hobby than a science. Today's dating techniques include methods introduced recently by microbiology, the study of living or once-living cells and genes—particles so small that they can be seen only with a powerful microscope. These techniques, which we shall discuss in the next chapter, help scientists find out not only the age of mummies, but what the people ate, what diseases they may have had, their movement from place to place, and how they lived. At their conference, the scientists had twenty-five mummies from six hundred to seven thousand years old to study.

Not all natural mummies come from hot, dry lands. On September 19, 1991, some hikers in the Alps near the border between Italy and Austria came upon a very strange sight—the head and shoulders of a man sticking out from a melting glacier. They notified mountaineers who had removed other bodies from glaciers; these men realized this was not a recent death. This shriveled body was very old, and so were the clothing and articles found with it—a leather quiver with fourteen arrows, a flint for striking fire, and an ax with a metal head, among other things.

Scientists called in to see and remove the body, which had been mummified by wind and freezing, were puzzled and amazed. Newspaper reporters immediately named the corpse "Iceman." Just over five feet tall, he wore a finely stitched leather suit padded with hay for insulation and leather shoes stuffed with grass for extra warmth. He had a small, polished, doughnut-shaped stone with a string tassel on a leather thong about his neck.

The first carbon tests of the hay insulation in his clothing indicated that the Iceman was 4,600 to 4,800 years old, which meant he lived in the Early Bronze Age. But then more careful tests made a little later at the University of Innsbruck showed that he was much older, between 4,931 and 5,477 years old, which meant he lived during the Late Stone Age, or almost 3,500 years B.C. His ax, which at first was thought to be bronze, proved on examination to be pure copper, further evidence of the earlier date. Scientists say this is the oldest and best-preserved specimen of early man ever found.

Soon after the Iceman arrived at Innsbruck, his body was bathed with fungicide, wrapped in a sterile plastic sheet, covered with chipped ice, and stored in a refrigerated room with temperature and humidity that match those of the glacier where he was found. The mummy is removed only for thirty-minute periods of time when specific tests are to be made. His skin, bones, fingernails, and internal organs are intact. Of special interest are three tattoos on his lower spine, right ankle, and behind his left knee; until this discovery, scientists thought the first tattoos appeared 2,500 years later.

The scientists in charge of the Iceman make every effort to let other scientists from all over the world share in their research, even providing small bits of material and body tissue for their analysis. Studies by the methods of microbiology are expected to reveal much more as these methods are improved. Care for the Iceman costs ten thousand dollars a month, but scientists think this unique opportunity to study the ancient mummy first-hand is well worth the expense.

Human skeletons and parts of skeletons found in many different parts of the world are also important clues for scientists who study the ancient past

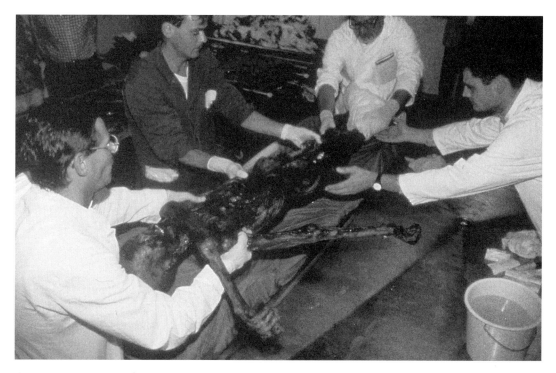

Scientists examining the Iceman COURTESY GERHARD HUNTER LEITNER/GAMMA

of human beings. People have always wondered when and where and how mankind first appeared on earth. Myths and speculation have led to extensive scientific study and investigation, but even today there are almost as many theories as there are "experts" in the field. With so much digging going on all over the world, it's not surprising that almost every month some "new" skeleton is found in some unexpected place. The study of bones, many of which are fossilized, and especially artifacts found with the bones, adds to the understanding of our own beginning. Often the new finding creates more puzzles than it solves.

One of the biggest puzzles among experts is the relationship between the Neanderthals and Cro-Magnon peoples, both of whom lived in the Middle East, parts of Europe, and Northern Africa at roughly the same time, some

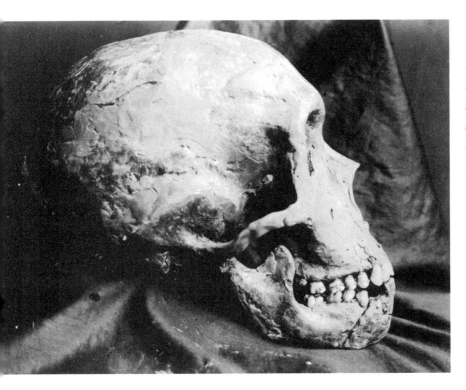

Big-boned Neanderthals had a sloping forehead and heavy jaw.
COURTESY AMERICAN MUSEUM OF NATURAL HISTORY, NEG. # 125964

fifty thousand to one hundred thousand years ago. The beetle-browed Neanderthals with their massive bones were until recently thought to be brutes, big in physical strength but lacking in intelligence. They became extinct about thirty-five thousand years ago. The slender, small-boned, and presumably much more intelligent Cro-Magnons are our ancient ancestors. The big question has been whether the Cro-Magnons evolved from the Neanderthals, or whether the two groups lived in different places and migrated to the same area. If the latter was the case, did the Neanderthals simply die off because they were too stupid to adapt to changing conditions? Did the Cro-Magnons make better weapons, outsmart the Neanderthals, and destroy them? Or did the two groups communicate with each other, perhaps mate with each other, and eventually produce modern man?

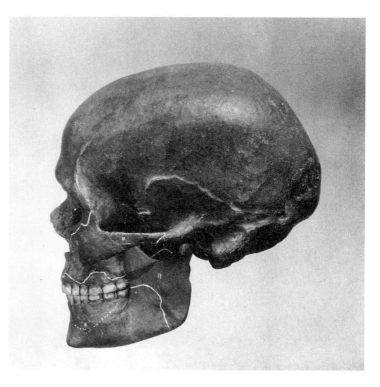

Cro-Magnons had a full, rounded forehead and delicate bones.
COURTESY AMERICAN MUSEUM OF NATURAL HISTORY, NEG. # 310705

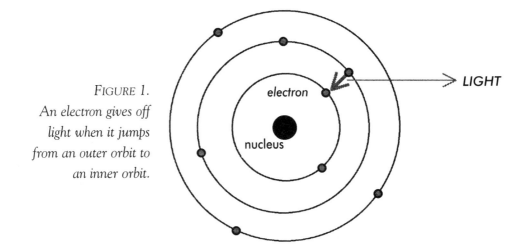

FIGURE 1.
An electron gives off
light when it jumps
from an outer orbit to
an inner orbit.

Scientists agreed that knowing *when* these people were living and evolving could be a great help in understanding their relationships. Carbon dating tells age back to about forty thousand years, and potassium-argon dating—another method that we shall discuss later—dates fossils older than half a million years. But until recently there has been no way to date objects from the period in between, the period during which modern man evolved. Then in the late 1980s scientists developed a new method, *thermoluminescence*, to date artifacts from this period.

What is thermoluminescence, and how does it work? *Thermo* is a Greek word meaning "heat," as in "thermometer." *Lumin* is from a Latin word meaning "light," and appears in such English words as "luminous" and "illuminate." So thermoluminescence must deal with heat and light.

We have learned that atoms consist of a nucleus surrounded by orbiting electrons, somewhat like planets orbiting the sun. Unlike the planets, however, electrons can move only in certain distinct orbits, as shown in Figure 1.

When an electron jumps from an *outer* orbit to one of the *inner* orbits, it gives off light. But if atoms are bombarded by radiation from some radioactive element, the energy of the bombardment knocks an electron from one of the *inner* orbits to one of the *outer* orbits.

Most materials—clay, for example—contain small amounts of radioactive elements such as uranium or thorium. So some of the atoms of substances in clay have their electrons knocked into outer orbits. When clay pottery is fired in a kiln to make it hard and durable, the electrons that were knocked into outer orbits fall back into lower orbits. Thus, firing the clay "resets the clock" to zero.

After the clay has cooled, the radioactive elements again start knocking electrons into outer orbits. As time passes, the number of electrons in outer

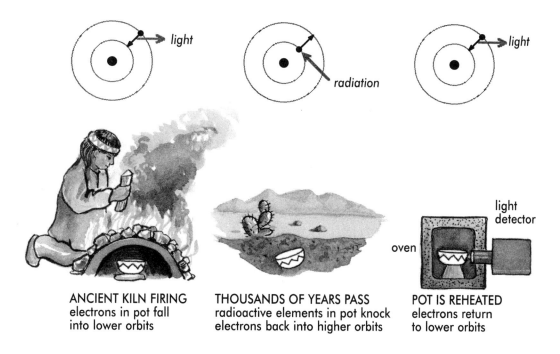

ANCIENT KILN FIRING
electrons in pot fall
into lower orbits

THOUSANDS OF YEARS PASS
radioactive elements in pot knock
electrons back into higher orbits

POT IS REHEATED
electrons return
to lower orbits

FIGURE 2. *Clay pot and thermoluminescence dating.*

orbits increases very slowly but steadily. So if we heat an ancient clay pot or sherd in an oven, electrons once again fall back into lower orbits. As they do, they give off tiny amounts of light. The amount of light given off is a measure of how long ago the pot was fired. This process of heating the clay pot and carefully measuring the amount of light emitted is the basis of thermoluminescence dating. It provides a way to measure the age of artifacts like pieces of pottery that were fired as long ago as ninety thousand years, and helps to fill in information about an earlier period than carbon dating can reveal.

A fossilized skeleton that researchers have named Moshe was found in a cave called Kebera, in Israel. Although the head is missing, it is the one most nearly complete source of information about the structure and appearance of Neanderthals. Thermoluminescence dating of artifacts found with Moshe revealed his age to be about sixty thousand years—a time when Neanderthals were thought to inhabit the area. But then to the experts' surprise, thermoluminescence dating of artifacts found with "modern" Cro-Magnon skeletons in another cave a short distance from Kebera showed *these* skeletons to be about ninety-two thousand years old—more than thirty thousand years *older* than Moshe!

This information upsets some of the scientists' most cherished theories. The Neanderthals are evidently more "modern" than the experts believed.

Chapter 8

FINGERPRINTS AND ANCIENT BLOOD

Some scientists study the rich history and prehistory of people who lived in Asia, Africa, and Europe. Others are more interested in the peoples who first inhabited the Western Hemisphere. When and how did human beings first appear in the Americas? The generally accepted theory is that ancient Asians crossed into North America during the Ice Age, via a land bridge that linked Siberia and Alaska. In the 1920s, archaeologists found beautifully chipped stone spear and arrow points embedded in the ribs of species of bison that became extinct near the end of the Ice Age. In the 1940s, carbon dating of some of these ribs that had been found in north-western Canada showed them to be 11,500 years old, and scientists thought this was probably about the beginning of human habitation in North America.

Both amateur and professional scientists have presented evidence of earlier dates from time to time, but either the evidence was faulty or proof of the date was lacking. Then in early 1992, Richard MacNeish, of the Andover Foundation for Archaeological Research, in Massachusetts, reported finding human palm and fingerprints on clay in a cave on the grounds of Fort Bliss, New Mexico. The cave, in a limestone bluff, contains twenty-five distinct layers that range from modern times at the top to ancient times at the bottom.

Fireplaces surrounded by heat-cracked stones appeared in many of the layers. Some contained logs up to eight inches in diameter—much too large to have been dragged in by animals. Only people could have carried or rolled them there. The handprints, verified as human, were on clay that had been shaped for a fire pit and hardened by the fire. Carbon dating of the logs and charcoal in the fireplaces, confirmed by thermoluminescence dating of the clay, showed the prints to be twenty-eight thousand, perhaps thirty-eight thousand, years old!

What can it mean except that human beings lived in North America long before the end of the Ice Age? Will someone uncover even older evidence? Perhaps. More and more people with some knowledge of archaeology are exploring places that no one has explored before, and a few of their discoveries have disproved widely accepted theories. For example, anthropologists had believed that the tropical rain forests of Central and South America were too fragile and had too few natural resources to support a large human population. But now there is growing evidence that in fact some of the oldest and most developed civilizations in the Western Hemisphere had their origin along the banks of the Amazon River in the heart of a Brazilian rain forest. In 1990, a team of anthropologists headed by Anna C. Roosevelt of the Field Museum of Natural History in Chicago found reddish brown pottery sherds and other artifacts deep in the interior of Brazil. Thermoluminescence dating showed the pieces to be eight thousand years old. This is three thousand years older than the oldest pottery previously discovered in regions along the coast, which were thought to be the sites of the earliest civilizations.

Some of the commonest evidence of early human activity is the artwork found on walls of caves. All over the world, both amateur and professional scientists have found hundreds of paintings and carvings of animals, people, and various objects, or simply symbols scratched on the rock. Unlike the pictures hidden deep in the Lascaux Cave, which we mentioned in Chapter 1, most of this artwork is out in the open, where any passerby can see it. Some of the art is crude; some is very beautiful and elaborate. All of it rouses curiosity and speculation about the artists.

Among the finest and most unusual specimens of rock art in the

These pottery sherds from Brazil are eight thousand years old. COURTESY FIELD MUSEUM OF NATURAL HISTORY, NEG. # 111811

Western Hemisphere are paintings on the walls of limestone caves and overhangs along the banks of the Pecos River in southwest Texas. Analysis of artifacts found in the caves and carbon dating of charcoal showed that hunter-gatherers had lived there from about 5000 B.C. until the Spanish entered the area in the sixteenth century. But no one could be sure when the paintings were made. Experts who studied the style and subjects depicted estimated that they were between 3,200 and 4,000 years old.

But today's scientists have developed tools and technologies unknown until very recently. Anthropologists had known for some time that early artists mixed binders of blood, urine, honey, and other organic substances into their paint pigments. So the paint could be carbon dated—except for the troublesome fact that no one could see a way to separate the carbon in the paint from the carbon in the rock on which the paint was applied.

To solve this problem, anthropologist Harry Shafer of Texas A & M University asked for help from Marvin Rowe, a chemistry professor there. Rowe was an expert in dating meteorites and other objects from outer space. He said he was more at home measuring the age of objects in billions rather than thousands of years, but the project intrigued him.

With help from two other chemists, he used new advances in chemistry to separate organic substances in the paint from the underlying rock. Gathering chips of paint that had flaked off the walls, the chemists carefully burned the flakes, producing a tiny amount of smoke that contained carbon dioxide and other chemicals. Then using a mass spectrometer, a new kind of device that we shall discuss in a moment, the chemists were able to find the ratio of carbon 14 atoms and stable carbon 12, and thus carbon-date the paint.

Their results showed the paintings to be 3,865 years old, give or take a hundred years. This confirmed the anthropologists' estimate but narrowed the time span by nearly a thousand years. Later this team of chemists used the same technique to date older cave paintings in Brazil, with equally good results. As other cave art comes to light—older perhaps than the handprints found in New Mexico—the chemists are now prepared to analyze and date it.

The mass spectrometer is one of the most valuable tools for carbon dating. As we said earlier, when carbon dating was first introduced, scientists needed a lump of material about the size of a walnut to perform the test. But often an excavation did not yield a lump big enough for analysis. Or worse, obtaining a walnut-size lump might largely destroy a valuable artifact such as a small carved bone figure or a textile fragment. But with a mass spectrometer, dust-size specimens are more than large enough for testing.

A mass spectrometer is to atoms what a prism is to light. If we shine white light into the face of a prism, the light emerging from the other face consists of a full "rainbow" of colors, with each color emerging at a different angle from the prism. The prism separates the white light into all of its component colors.

In the same sense, a mass spectrometer separates a mixture of different kinds of atoms into separate "piles" of atoms of the same kind. As Figure 1 shows, the material to be analyzed is placed in an oven and heated until it turns into gas. The gas then enters a chamber where the atoms are bombarded by radiation that knocks away the electrons surrounding the nucleus of each atom. This leaves each atom with a positive charge. Next, these charged atoms, called *ions*, are directed toward a magnet, as the figure shows. The magnetic field of the magnet plays the role that a prism plays in separating light. An ordinary atom would sail right through the magnetic field, but the ions, being positively charged, are deflected as they enter the magnetic field.

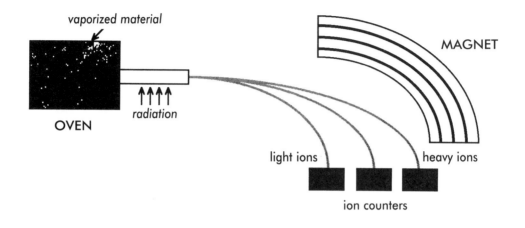

FIGURE 1. *A mass spectrometer separates different kinds of atoms from each other.*

As we know, each kind of atom has its own mass or weight. That is, each kind has a specific number of protons and neutrons in its nucleus. The heavier an atom is, the less the magnetic field deflects it. So the different kinds of atoms emerge from the magnetic field neatly separated according to weight. Counting devices then record the number of each kind of atom.

In the early 1990s, a very young science, molecular biology, introduced a new idea for finding the age of some very old things. Using highly specialized techniques and extremely sensitive instruments, scientists analyze tiny specks of blood taken from spear and arrow points and flint tools, as well as other sources. By examining even ancient samples, they can tell whether the blood is human or animal—and what kind of animal. When they determine the age of the spear point or tool stained by the blood, they also know the age of the blood. One of the oldest objects studied thus far is a flint tool stained with human blood. It was found in Iraq and may be two hundred thousand years old.

Molecular biologists can identify and analyze the DNA of the blood specimen. DNA is the chemical basis of heredity found in every cell of living creatures. It's the specific code or combination of genes that make up the blueprint of every human being, animal, or insect. Although each pattern is distinct and different from all others, family characteristics such as eye and hair color or physical weaknesses or peculiarities can be identified. DNA samples may come from blood or any protein tissue such as dried skin or flesh from mummies. Since every cell contains the complete pattern, dust-size particles are large enough for analysis.

DNA loses nothing through aging, so anthropologists believe it may become important evidence in tracing the development and travels of ancient peoples and animals. It could be possible, for example, to identify present-day descendants of the Iceman, discussed in the chapter on mummies. And scientists with enough specimens to study could solve the mysteries of origins and migrations of the Neanderthal and Cro-Magnon peoples.

This science is growing so fast that even the experts find it hard to keep up. One of the pioneers, Thomas Loy of the Australian National University in Canberra, said in 1992, "Four years ago I thought it would take a hundred years to look for DNA in Neanderthal blood. Now I'm starting to look for those genes. That's how fast the technology has advanced."

The technology that has brought this rapid growth is a process called *polymerase chain reaction*, or simply PCR. Somewhat like a copy machine, a PCR machine can make millions of copies of a single gene in half an hour, and supply researchers with all the DNA they need for their studies. PCR is available in simple, inexpensive machines for use by drug companies, criminal investigation labs, and science labs all over the world.

The techniques of microbiology have captured the imagination of people outside the realm of science. Michael Crichton's book *Jurassic Park* and

Steven Spielberg's movie version of the book grew from the idea of collecting dinosaur blood from a fossilized insect that had sucked the blood from a dinosaur, and then using the dinosaur DNA to clone enough cells to create a whole, living dinosaur. This, of course, is pure fantasy, and not even a remote goal for scientists. Nevertheless, some scientist *has* found at least one very ancient insect preserved in a blob of amber. Who knows what may happen next?

Chapter 9

THE MYSTERY OF THE MONSTERS

Millions of years before there were any living things on Earth, there were rocks—*igneous* rocks formed from the Earth's molten interior. Over more millions of years the wind and water, freezing and thawing, eroded the rocks, forming sand. The sand washed into riverbeds and the seas, where the tremendous pressure of layer upon layer slowly formed it into a second kind of rock—*sedimentary* rock—sometimes hundreds of feet thick and thousands of square miles in area.

Inside the Earth, tremendous forces constantly reshaped Earth's surface. Rocks that had been flat seabeds were pushed up into mountain ranges thousands of miles long. Layers of sedimentary rocks, now well above sea level, were buckled, folded, fractured, and sometimes stood on edge or overturned. The various layers, each laid down at a different period and under different conditions, were often easy to distinguish, with distinct lines between layers. Color, texture, hardness, and composition varied from one layer to another.

As scientists studied the ancient rocks, they noticed that cross sections of sedimentary rocks from one location matched cross sections from other locations, even on different continents. In the 1960s they began to realize that the surface of the Earth is not continuous, but is made of a number of gigantic slabs, or *plates*, some as large as whole continents, floating on a sea of partially molten rock. Over many aeons, churning of the underlying molten rock pushed the plates around, often to places thousands of miles from their original locations. Some scientists observed that western coastlines of some continents, if pushed across an ocean, would fit quite well with the eastern coastlines of other continents. For this reason and others, including the matching layers of sedimentary rocks in separate continents, they concluded that at one time in the very distant past, there must have been just one enormous land mass.

Some of the first geologists to study these things realized that the lowest layers of sedimentary rocks were the oldest and those nearest the surface were youngest. So they had some idea of the *relative* ages of the layers, but how could they find out anything about the *absolute* ages?

The answer turned out to be similar in method to carbon dating. Along the edges of the plates, the underlying molten rock sometimes pushed upward, creating islands. Often the islands emerge as fuming volcanoes, spilling molten rock, or *lava*, that flows over the sides of the volcanoes, building them ever higher. Other volcanoes erupt where the plates are thin, again spilling lava and ashes around them. The lava and ash flows are the key to revealing the age of the various kinds of rock we find on Earth.

A core of rock removed from the Earth shows cross sections of the various layers of sedimentary rock, and often a layer of hardened volcanic material. When a volcano erupts, the lava and ashes contain radioactive potassium, which decays slowly with a particular half-life into argon gas. At the time of the volcanic eruption, the hot lava and ash boil off any argon present in them. So when the lava and ash first cool and solidify, they contain no argon, and only radioactive potassium. But then as the potassium continues to decay into argon, the argon is trapped in the lava and ash. By measuring the ratio of argon to radioactive potassium in a layer of volcanic material, scientists can estimate the age of the sedimentary rock layers both above and below the lava and ash. For example, if the dating shows the volcanic layer is 65 million years old, the rock layer just below it is a little more than 65 million years old; and the rock layer just above it is a little less than 65 million years old. (See Figure 1.)

Many thousands of volcanic eruptions have taken place all over the Earth from practically the time when the Earth was formed up to the present. So scientists have been able to piece together a geologic calendar for the various layers of sedimentary rocks found all over the Earth. The lava and ash layers provide an index that geologists used to divide Earth's rock formations into *eras*, and each era into *periods*. By identifying and naming

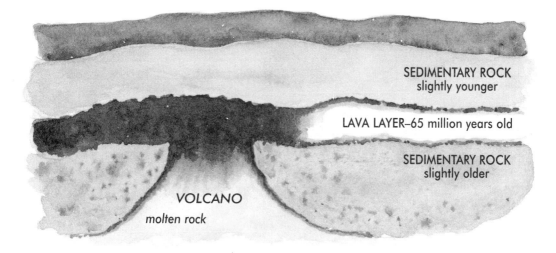

FIGURE 1. *Measuring the ratio of argon and radioactive potassium in a layer of volcanic material between two layers of sedimentary rock helps scientists estimate the age of the sedimentary rocks.*

these divisions, they made a universal timescale that everyone can use as a reference. (See Figure 2.)

About two hundred years ago, geologists began to find fossils of living things in various rock layers from the Paleozoic era, which began about 600 million years ago. By this time, the Earth had reached about 90 percent of its present age. The oldest of the Paleozoic layers hold plant fossils— imprints of seaweeds and mosses—and the simplest animal forms, such as worms, jellyfish, and shellfish.

Younger rock layers hold more and larger plant life—palmlike plants as tall as trees—and the first animals with backbones—fish, birds, amphibians, and reptiles. And dinosaurs. Many kinds and sizes of dinosaurs, some as small as a rabbit, some fifty feet long that weighed many tons.

For 160 million years, all kinds of dinosaurs flourished all over the Earth. Their fossils are found on every continent, even Antarctica. Many of the fossils found in one part of the Earth are the same kind as those found on other continents. And then about 65 million years ago, in a period as short as one hundred thousand years—a mere moment in geologic time—they all disappeared. What could have happened to them?

There have been many theories and much speculation. Enormous geologic changes took place during the last 25 million years of the Mesozoic era. The continents were formed. Mountain ranges with peaks several miles high took shape. Inland seas drained away into the oceans. Some scientists who study dinosaurs think that Earth's climate became too cold for them. Without fur or feathers to keep them warm, and too big to burrow into the mud, they simply froze to death. Other scientists note that the earliest dinosaur eggs had thicker shells than those of the last five million years of dinosaur habitation. Perhaps other animals—even the first mammals, which may have been smarter than the dinosaurs—ate all the dinosaur eggs.

Another theory was that they were poisoned by eating flowering plants,

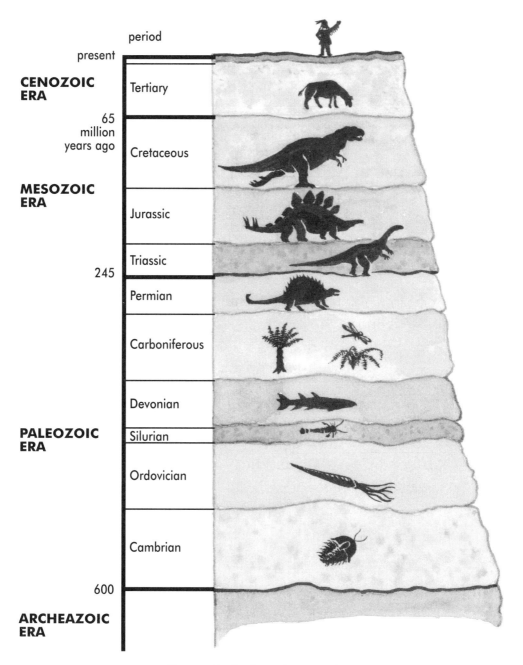

FIGURE 2. *Geological time scale*

but flowering plants were abundant 50 million years before the dinosaurs disappeared. Some scientists speculated that a nearby star exploded and showered the Earth with radiation that killed the dinosaurs. But if this was the answer, why didn't all the other animals also die?

Still other scientists proposed one more "outer space" solution. Perhaps, they said, a comet or a meteor had struck the Earth. The impact would have raised a huge cloud of dust that would have enveloped the whole planet, shutting off light and warmth from the sun for many months. All plant life would have died, and without plant food, the dinosaurs all died. But again, why just the dinosaurs?

As a matter of fact, scientists now know that about 75 percent of all the plants and animals alive at that time did disappear. But most scientists believed that the disappearancc was due to natural causes such as climate changes.

In the late 1970s, two American scientists, Luis Alvarez and his son Walter, were investigating a thin layer of clay deposited about 65 million years ago near the medieval town of Gubbio in northern Italy. Much to their surprise, they discovered that it contained the rare element iridium in concentrations more than a hundred times greater than normal. They knew that most of the iridium on Earth had originally come from meteorites, so they suggested that a huge meteorite had struck the Earth 65 million years ago. If this was true, they said, the entire Earth should be covered with a thin layer of iridium dust laid down 65 million years ago. From the amount of iridium they found in Italy, they estimated that the meteor would have been about six miles in diameter, and its impact would have created a crater at least a hundred miles wide. The impact, equal to millions of exploding hydrogen bombs, would have hurled into the atmosphere trillions of tons of material, which would have taken many months to settle back to Earth. During that time, the sky would have been black with dust that blocked the sun's heat and light from the Earth.

The Alvarezes realized that without heat and light, plants would stop growing. There would be nothing for plant-eating animals to eat. This would have set off a chain of events leading, they proposed, to the disappearance of many plants and animals 65 million years ago.

At first most scientists were skeptical. It was generally believed that changes in nature were slow, not sudden. And where, they asked, was the crater? But a few scientists pointed out that nearly 70 percent of the Earth's

Luis and Walter Alvarez point out the iridium layer found throughout the Earth.
COURTESY OF UNIVERSITY OF CALIFORNIA LAWRENCE BERKELEY LABORATORY

surface is covered with water; so it was likely that any crater would be at the bottom of some ocean.

It was also difficult to check the prediction that a worldwide layer of iridium dust would be found. Much of the material dating back 65 million years had been eroded away, and again there was the problem of the oceans. The continual motion of the plates had buckled, shifted, and destroyed about 25 percent of the ocean floor that had been there 65 million years ago.

But slowly the evidence began to accumulate. One of the first important finds was made in New Mexico, where the iridium-bearing clay level was discovered at a depth of eight hundred feet. By 1987, the layer had been found in dozens of locations at various places over the surface of the Earth. Even more interesting, the layer contained bits of compressed quartz and tiny glass beads. The beads, of various shapes and about the size of sugar crystals, scientists believed had been created by some gigantic blow. The intense heat of the impact had melted bits of earth into glass. Some beads found in Haiti were as large as grains of sand. Scientists believed these must have come from a nearby explosion because they were too heavy to have traveled very far through the air.

In 1980, geologists exploring for oil off the north coast of the Yucatán Peninsula discovered a circular formation almost exactly one hundred miles in diameter. But they did not know of the Alvarezes' theory, so their discovery did not come to light until 1990. Further work showed that the formation was indeed a crater, but was it a 65-million-year-old crater?

The answer could be clinched if the glass beads and other once-molten but now hardened rock near the crater proved to be the same age and composition as the material in the crater. But this was no easy fact to establish. First, there was very little of the bead-bearing material available from the Haiti site. And second, impact craters are hard to date because they remain hot for a long time after the impact, and this changes the materials in them that need to be dated. But in spite of these difficulties, the work all came together in 1992 with a combination of luck and an improved version of the potassium-argon dating technique.

In the old technique, the material to be dated was split into two pieces, and different methods were used to analyze them. One piece was analyzed chemically for its potassium content, and the other was melted to extract the argon. The ratio of argon to potassium was worked out from the results of the two measurements, giving an age for the material. This method had two big difficulties. First, there was no certainty that the ratio of argon to potassium was the same in both pieces. Second, because argon is a gas, it was difficult to extract it completely from a sample. So an incorrect date could result. It would be much better to use the same test for both pieces.

With the new technique, a sample is first bombarded with neutrons, a process that converts the potassium into a different isotope of argon—argon 39. The argon in the sample caused by natural potassium decay is the isotope argon 40. The argon 39 is a measure of how much potassium was originally in the sample; so the ratio of argon 39 to argon 40 provides a date for the material from just one sample. Since argon 39 and argon 40 are both gases, the same process can be used to measure the amount of both; the ratio remains the same whether very small or large amounts of argon are extracted. Very small amounts can even be boiled off by using laser beams.

After much searching, samples of material that could be analyzed were finally found in two drill holes in the crater. The new analysis method established that the date of the impact was almost exactly 65.1 million years ago. The same method used to analyze the larger glass beads found in Haiti proved them also to be 65.1 million years old. Analysis of the material taken from the crater and from Haiti showed that both came from limestone. There could be little doubt—an enormous meteor had hit Earth 65.1 million years ago, spewing vast amounts of material into Earth's atmosphere.

But scientists continued to disagree about whether the meteor strike by itself was enough to destroy 75 percent of the Earth's plant and animal life. Some believed that other factors were at work and that the meteor impact was the final blow. Even Walter Alvarez said, "If a single big impact and a single big extinction was the whole story, it would be clear by now."

Then in 1993, Dr. Virgil L. Sharpton and other scientists from the Planetary and Lunar Institute in Houston, Texas, made new measurements of the crater, now called the Chicxulub impact crater, and found that it is 50 percent larger than the earlier measurements showed it to be. It's 186 miles across and more than six miles deep. Sharpton says the impact would have created temperatures of more than twenty-thousand degrees, sent four-hundred-foot tidal waves roaring across the ocean, and triggered huge earthquakes hundreds of miles away. Although the new measurements strengthen the theory that the meteor impact wiped out the dinosaurs, many geologists and other experts still believe that other factors were also responsible.

Had such a collision ever happened before? Could it happen again? Recent evidence shows that another mass extinction of plant and animal life some 370 million years ago was probably related to a meteor impact. Again tiny glass beads dating back to that time have been found. The story is still unfolding, but there can be little doubt that objects from outer space have played a very important role in the evolution of life and of Earth itself.

As to the likelihood that such an event may happen again, the odds are not very good. Scientists today know a great deal about the comets, meteors, and other bodies whizzing around in outer space. They know where these bodies are, the paths they are following, and how fast they travel. Some scientists have suggested plans for blowing up a comet or meteor while it's still out in space if it should be zeroing in on Earth.

Chapter 10

MOON ROCKS AND METEORS

How old is our planet Earth, and how did it begin? Probably people have wondered ever since there were people *to* wonder. One early theorist who made a serious effort to establish the age of the Earth was Bishop Ussher, who lived in seventeenth-century Ireland. His information source was the Bible, which gives a detailed account of Earth's creation as well as the many generations that followed Adam and Eve. The bishop painstakingly studied the lists of kings and judges in the Old Testament and concluded that the Earth was created in the year 4004 B.C.

In another part of the world with a different religious background, people in India believed that the Earth had no beginning—that it had always existed. This eternity was sometimes represented as a snake swallowing its tail, along with the legend "My end is my beginning."

A few years after Bishop Ussher's estimate, a Scottish geologist, James Hutton, made one of the first scientific attempts to date the age of Earth. He decided it must be at least a few million years old to account for the deep gorges cut by rivers and the ground-down look of many mountains.

Another estimate was that the Earth was about 90 million years old because it would have taken the rains, streams, and rivers that long to dissolve enough salt from the rocks and land to make the oceans as salty as they are.

In the eighteenth century a French scientist figured that the Earth was about seventy-five thousand years old. It would have taken that long, he thought, to cool from what he assumed began as a hot, molten mass. Later, in the nineteenth century, an English scientist calculated that it would have taken the Earth 25 to 100 million years to cool. But of course no one had any idea how hot it was to start with. And besides, wasn't it the Earth even before it cooled?

Such speculations proved to be useless, and most scientists today believe the Earth did not start as a molten mass. But finding the age of the Earth was obviously no simple task.

It was not until the end of the nineteenth century that any really good estimates could be made. In 1896 a French scientist, Antoine-Henri Becquerel, discovered radioactivity. Here, as we've learned, is the secret for dating. Very soon after his discovery, scientists realized that the ratio of lead to uranium—which is radioactive and decays to lead—becomes larger and larger for older and older rocks. So if they could work out the rate of decay—that is, if they could find the half-life of uranium—it should be possible to estimate the age of a rock.

Research revealed two kinds of uranium, one with a half-life of about 700 million years, and another with a half-life of about 4.5 billion years. Both are useful in dating the age of the Earth because they have such long half-lives.

So what is the age of the Earth based on radioactive dating? The answer is 4.6 billion years, give or take a hundred million years. But the answer is not as simple as dating a few old rocks in the backyard, or even the oldest rocks anyone has been able to find. What scientists accept as the age of the Earth depends on what they believe and have found out about how the Earth was formed. As with most scientific theories, there are numerous pieces of evidence from many different sources pointing to the same explanation.

Scientists have known a number of things about the Earth for a long time. First, the Earth and its atmosphere are made up of many different elements. Some, like hydrogen, are light; others, like gold, are heavy. Second, studies of earthquake tremors reveal that the Earth has an inner metallic core. The core is surrounded by a thick, partly molten but rocky shell, fairly rich in metals, called the *mantle*. And finally, there is a relatively thin outer crust about twenty miles thick—the part we live on. (See Figure 1.)

The crust is not one continuous layer like the shell of an egg, but is broken up into large pieces called plates, as we discussed in the previous chapter, which float on the molten rock of the mantle. The crust is very

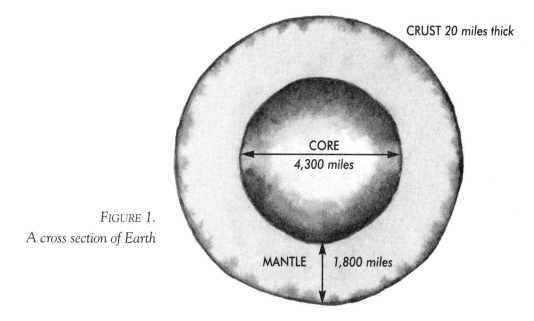

CRUST 20 miles thick

CORE
4,300 miles

MANTLE | 1,800 miles

FIGURE 1.
A cross section of Earth

rocky and contains little metal compared to the core and the mantle. That is why silver and gold are so precious.

How can science account for the metals and rocks that form the Earth? To find the answer, geologists and astronomers looked outward to the stars. They found that basically there are two kinds of stars. One kind, called *first-generation stars*, contains mostly hydrogen and helium. The other kind, *second-generation stars*, contains not only hydrogen and helium but also heavier elements such as carbon and iron. Our own Sun is a second-generation star. This fact was an important clue to explaining the formation of the Earth, which also contains both light and heavy elements. Probably the Earth and the Sun, and the rest of the planets in our solar system, were created about the same time from the same material.

First-generation stars were formed from hydrogen and helium gas created at the time of the origin of the universe. The pressure and heat were so great in the interior of these stars that nuclear reactions in them created new, heavier elements such as oxygen, carbon, and iron. But even at these extreme pressures and temperatures, iron was the heaviest metal formed.

As some first-generation stars grew old, they finally exploded; and in this process elements heavier than iron, such as gold and uranium, were formed. After these explosions, space was filled with a mixture of hydrogen, helium, and the heavier elements created by the heat and pressure of the explosions. It is this "dust" from the explosion of first-generation stars that provides the raw material for our own solar system. And that includes us. We can say we are literally made of star dust!

How our solar system formed from this ancient dust is not entirely understood. But it seems likely that the explosion of a nearby star sent a shock wave through the dust of our future solar system that caused it to form lumps here and there. Some of these lumps grew to even bigger lumps as the pull of their gravity collected more and more of the small lumps. As time passed and the process continued, some of the lumps grew to enormous sizes, forming Earth and the other planets in our solar system.

Because of the heat created by the extreme pressure in their interiors, the huge lumps began to soften. Heavy metals such as iron and uranium sank to the center, and the lighter rocky materials such as basalt and granite floated to the top. Between the interior and the outer surface, mixtures of metals and rock formed.

Some of these lumps collided with other lumps, shattering them into fragments of metal, rock, and metal-rock mixtures. Scientists believe that the meteorites that have fallen to Earth since then are pieces of these shattered lumps formed at the time our solar system was created. This is because most meteorites are metallic, rocky, or a mixture of rocks and metals. Radioactive dating of these meteorites gives an age of about 4.6 billion years.

Earth kept on growing as it continually collided with thousands and thousands of smaller lumps. This almost constant bombardment probably melted the surface, so that Earth's first ocean was one vast sea of molten rock. Finally, as more and more lumps became part of Earth and other planets, there were fewer and fewer collisions. Earth's surface began to cool and form a solid crust.

Earthquakes and volcanic eruptions generated in Earth's hot interior continually broke and shifted the crust. Later, as Earth's atmosphere formed, wind and rain eroded the surface. Earthquakes and volcanic eruptions were fewer, but they continued to help shape Earth's surface.

With all this turmoil over millions of years, it seemed unlikely that any of the original rock created at the time of the Earth's formation would ever be found. And this seems to be true. Most of the oldest rocks found on Earth date back about 3.9 billion years.

Scientists began to realize that our nearest heavenly neighbor, the Moon, was an important clue in the story of the formation and age of the solar system. It seemed likely that the Moon, being much less massive than Earth, might have kept much of the original rock formed from the ancient dust. The Moon's smaller mass is important for several reasons. For one thing, because of its smaller gravitational pull it would not have collided with so many other lumps of primitive matter. Second, a smaller size would mean less interior pressure; so volcanic eruptions and earthquakes would be less frequent. And finally, no atmosphere would form, since there would not be enough gravity to keep the gases from escaping into space. And of course without an atmosphere there are no winds and rainstorms to erode the Moon's surface.

So scientists looked forward with great anticipation to dating the first rocks the astronauts brought back from the Moon in 1968. This was a very delicate process. When the astronauts collected the rocks from the Moon's surface, they placed them in double Teflon bags to minimize contamination from outside. After the long journey back to Earth, the rocks were delivered to different laboratories for study. Here researchers removed the rocks from their bags and cleaned them with blasts of freon gas. Next they peeled away the outer rock layers with tungsten carbide chisels and stainless steel hammers, exposing a perfectly clean inner surface.

Next they used a sapphire mortar and pestle to crush a fragment of moon rock, and sifted the particles through a stainless steel mesh to separate the various kinds of minerals. Then they could examine individual mineral grains under a microscope and choose certain ones for further study. These they separated further according to hardness and magnetic properties. Finally they loaded one of the most radioactive samples, now reduced to the size of a pinhead or less, into a mass spectrometer, where it was vaporized into individual ions that could be counted by the spectrometer.

Moon rocks brought back to Earth by the Apollo 11 astronauts COURTESY NASA

What did research reveal about the age of the rocks? The oldest were 4.4 billion years old—not quite as old as the 4.6 billion-year-old meteorites found on Earth. But this difference is probably due to the fact that the oldest moon rocks were pulverized into dust by the heavy meteor bombardment in the early days of the solar system. The other important finding was that the moon rocks were made of much the same material as the stony meteorites and the mantle of the Earth. In fact, according to one theory, the Moon was formed from the debris when a huge asteroid collided with Earth some 20 million years after its formation.

About 4.3 billion years ago, Earth had cooled to the point where it was covered by a deep, warm ocean dotted here and there with volcanic

Scientists examine crushed moon rock enclosed in a sterile work area. COURTESY NASA

islands protruding above the ocean's surface. In another hundred million years or so, volcanic eruptions had created a dense atmosphere of carbon dioxide, water vapor, and other gases. Some of these gases—especially carbon dioxide, hydrogen, nitrogen, and oxygen—dissolved in the ocean, providing the raw materials of life.

Although we have only a crude understanding of the processes by which life emerged from these raw materials, there is fossil evidence of primitive organisms by 3.5 billion years ago. After that time, ever more complex organisms evolved, leaving their histories embedded in the sedimentary rocks, volcanic ashes, and lava flows we learned about in the previous chapter.

EPILOGUE

Finding out how old things are means searching for clues and looking for ways to solve puzzles. We have seen how scientists from different countries and different branches of science have used their expertise to add to the knowledge of the past. Some of their techniques, such as carbon dating and the use of CAT scans, have become commonplace. Others, such as analysis of ancient DNA, have barely begun to show what they have to offer.

New discoveries of things long hidden from view appear almost every week. Sometimes these discoveries help to confirm present theories, and sometimes they contradict them. Some ideas expressed in this book may soon prove to be wrong or out of date.

There is still much to learn about the age of things. Tree-ring scientists have a floating series of wood samples that will have to continue to float until someone finds a definite date at one end or the other for an anchor. Dinosaur specialists learn more all the time about dinosaurs. They know when the dinosaurs dominated life on Earth and when they became extinct. But no one knows how long individual dinosaurs lived, or how long it took a baby dinosaur to grow up to be an adult. People keep turning up all kinds of pieces of this and that from attics, abandoned buildings, old battlefields—almost everywhere; and one of the first things they want to know about these things is how old they are.

We hope that the chapters of this book will give readers an appreciation for the value of old and very old things. Everything is worth investigation, and people who truly appreciate the knowledge involved respect the value of what scientists are doing. Because of this they can understand why they should take great care never to harm or destroy anything that might prove of value—old trash heaps, old dwelling places, rock art. Once scarred or broken, the usefulness of one-of-a-kind things can be lost forever.

GLOSSARY

Absolute dating—*Determining the actual age of an object.*

Carbon 14 Dating—*The most common method for dating once-living plants and animals.*

CAT Scanner—*A computer-aided X-ray machine that can produce three-dimensional X rays.*

Dendrochronology—*The study of the growth of tree rings to date the age of a tree.*

Half-life—*The time it takes half the radioactive atoms in a substance to turn into nonradioactive atoms.*

Igneous Rocks—*Rocks formed from the Earth's molten interior.*

Isotope—*Atoms of the same element—uranium for example—that have different numbers of neutrons in their nuclei.*

Mass Spectrometer—*A device for counting the number of each of the different kinds of atoms in a substance.*

Potassium-Argon Dating—*One of the most useful methods for dating the age of volcanic ash and lava.*

Radioactive Decay—*A process whereby the radioactive atoms in a substance spontaneously decay into nonradioactive atoms.*

Relative Dating—*Determining the age of an object relative to some other object.*

Sedimentary Rocks—*Layers of rock formed by the settling of dust, sand, and rock particles suspended in air and water.*

Thermoluminescence Dating—*A method commonly used to date the age of pottery and other objects made from clay.*

Uranium Dating—*A common method for dating ancient rocks, based on the radioactive decay of uranium into lead.*

FOR FURTHER READING

Asimov, Isaac, and Janet Asimov. *Frontiers II: More Recent Discoveries about Life, Earth, Space, and the Universe.* New York: Truman Talley/Dutton, 1993. A collection of short scientific pieces published in the *Los Angeles Times* and elsewhere.

Denton, Michael. *The Dinosaur Encyclopedia.* New York: Simon and Schuster, 1992. A comprehensive, easy-to-understand book about all aspects of dinosaurs.

The Dorling Kindersley Encyclopedia. New York: Dorling Kindersley, 1993. A one-volume, well-illustrated, up-to-date encyclopedia providing background information on many of the subjects covered in this book.

El Mahdy, Christine. *Mummies, Myth and Magic in Ancient Egypt.* New York: Thames and Hudson, 1989. A well-rounded account of the role that mummies played in the life of ancient Egyptians, along with information about the techniques used to preserve mummies.

Farndon, John. *How the Earth Works.* Reader's Digest Assoc., 1992. A good introduction to the Earth's formation and evolution.

Romer, John. *Testament.* New York: Henry Holt, 1988. An archaeologist's account of the discovery of the Dead Sea Scrolls along with a discussion of how other archaeological findings are related to historical records in the Bible.

Sheets, Payson D. *The Ceren Site: A Prehistoric Village Buried by Volcanic Ash in Central America.* New York: Holt, Rinehart, and Winston, 1992. Dr. Sheets's own account of his discoveries and activities at Ceren.

INDEX

Page numbers for illustrations are in italics.